Bumfuzzle and Cattywampus:
Unlikely Detectives

Mystery at Rutherford Mansion

Alice Kanaka

This book is a work of fiction. The events, characters, and locations portrayed are imaginary. Their resemblance, if any, to real-life counterparts is entirely coincidental.

Table of Contents

Table of Contents

<u>**Other Books by Alice Kanaka**</u>

The Cardinal & The Crow
The Cardinal, The Fat Boy, & The Flamingo
The Cardinal & The Hawk

Bumfuzzle and Cattywampus: Unlikely Detectives
Trouble at the Buckeye Festival

<u>**Coming Soon**</u>

The Cardinal & The Crane

Bumfuzzle

Transitive verb. Chiefly dialectal: Confuse, Perplex, Fluster

Cattywampus

Adjective. Dialectal: Askew, Awry, Cater-cornered

Chapter 1

Marge looked up as lightning illuminated the dark, turreted, third story of Rutherford Mansion. The long-abandoned behemoth was rife with legends of curses and ghosts. Marge shivered and pulled her coat closely around her, stinkering twice. The frigid December wind pummeled her back and tossed her enormous, carrot-colored bun to and fro. Teeth chattering, she glanced at Joey to see how he was faring. "The airstream is excessively bitter for this season."

"I think we're in for a hard winter." He grimaced as he lifted one gloved hand at a time from his walker and flexed his fingers. He had replaced his customary cowboy hat with a ski cap to combat the wind and keep his ears warm. "Come on," he said, leaving the dirt path and plunging into the thick forest.

"I've never been to this locality, save that once we perambulated the milk plant," Marge mused.

The bruised clouds and dense pine canopy threw murky shadows across the bare, jagged branches of immense, winterized bushes. A thick blanket of decomposing leaves camouflaged treacherous roots and rocks lurking beneath. They moved cautiously, stepping around holes and periodically disentangling Joey's walker.

Marge started violently when a dirty but enthusiastic golden retriever appeared seemingly out of nowhere. Sniffing each of them in turn, he wagged his tail and led them toward the house. As they approached the mansion, the dog ran ahead and sniffed the bushes bordering the rear before running back to join them.

An enormous man carrying a shotgun stepped out of the trees, causing Marge to release a burst of nervous flatulence. "This is private property. You need to leave."

The dog whined, laid down, and covered his snout with his paws.

"Friends of ours are renting the house," Joey said. "Do you work for Mr. Rutherford?"

"Yeah, and he didn' say nothin' about renting."

"Perhaps you worked for the former Rutherford who recently passed away."

The man removed his hunting cap and ran a large, gloved hand over his bald head. "Guess I'd better get it sorted."

"Is this your dog?" Joey asked.

"What?" He glanced at the dog. "Nah, but he hangs round, so I feed 'im sometimes."

"Does he possess a moniker?"

The man stared blankly at Marge.

"A name?" Joey clarified.

"Dunno. Just call 'im Dog."

"Have you knowledge of the origin of these cavities?" She motioned toward the ground.

"Just kids messin' round," he grumbled.

"Do you live in the house?" Joey asked.

"Nah. Been empty as long as I remember. I've gotta get back to my rounds. Will you folks be here long?"

"We'll join the others around front." Joey nodded and turned his walker around.

"There's a road that ends in the driveway there, if you wanna drive next time."

"Thank you," Marge said, turning to follow Joey.

———⁂———

Joey paused after a few yards, looked back toward the clearing, and noticed the caretaker watching them with a frown. Marge collided with his stilled form and her foot descended into one of the holes, causing her to sit down hard.

Joey turned quickly to help her up as Dog snuffled her neck and tried to take a bite of her mammoth bun. Shooing him away, Joey said, "Are you hurt? Let me give you a hand."

"I'm undamaged." Marge's voice quivered. "It's fortunate that you curtailed my forward momentum, so my extremity was not twisted. I believe, however, that I alighted on an inflexible object."

"You landed on a rock?"

"Possibly." Marge nodded and felt underneath her. Pulling her foot out of the hole, she rolled onto her hands and knees, straightening her legs. "Observe, downward dog."

Joey chuckled, remembering Harriet's scandalized face when he first did the same in the Green, Buckwood's central park.

Marge stood and dusted off her ample derriere before gingerly testing her limbs for injury. "On subsequent visits, it might be prudent to heed the caretaker's advice and journey by automobile."

"You may be right. Either that or I need to buy an off-road walker. Are you sure you're okay?"

She slowly turned her head. "Where do you deduce the caretaker resides? Here on the estate? Was he in point of fact engaged by the Rutherfords?"

"We'll have to ask Hugh."

Joey stopped to study the blackened posterior of the building as they passed. "This must be where the kitchen fire started. I wonder if they'll be able to repair it." He glanced at Marge, who was unusually silent. "Penny for your thoughts."

"Do you deem James' request for assistance anomalous? For merely a rental agreement."

"He's very young and intimidated, I think, by Hugh Rutherford and the enormity of this place. You don't mind, do you?"

"No, I'm thrilled to glimpse the interior. I merely ruminated over our inclusion. The situation does appear atypical." She shook her head. "I do not demur." Rounding the corner of the building and catching sight of the front entrance, she stopped, transfixed.

The mansion was built in the style of a small French castle; the grand front entrance and enormous windows, although old and covered with dirt, displayed the highest levels of quality and craftmanship.

"Today is my preliminary observation of the fascia," she whispered. "Can you envisage its pinnacle?"

Joey scanned the long, circular drive and approached James' car. James and his new wife, Freida, got out of the car and greeted him and Marge as Hugh Rutherford, wearing blue jeans, a down jacket, and a hard hat opened the front door and headed toward the drive.

Sticking out a well-manicured hand and smiling with even, white teeth, Hugh welcomed them. "Good to see you. Is that your dog?"

"No, the caretaker said he just hangs around and that he feeds him sometimes."

"Cool," James said. "House with a dog."

"The caretaker?" Hugh looked perplexed. "I don't think I have a caretaker. What does he look like?"

"He's a large man, like James, but without the beard." Joey looked at Marge for confirmation.

"He's bald…" Her eyes rolled up as she tried to picture him. "Prominent nose, narrow lips, hunting vest."

"He also had on heavy boots and was carrying a shotgun."

Hugh nodded. "I'll keep an eye out for him." He turned toward the house. "The renovations have progressed more quickly than I anticipated. Are you on any kind of timeline?"

"We were hoping to move before the snow flies."

"Your apartment would be considerably warmer."

"Probably, but we're so cramped with both of our stuff in there, we can hardly walk from one room to another."

"You won't have that problem here." Hugh laughed. "Let me get you some hardhats, and I'll show you what we've done so far."

Handing out the hats, he led them up the stone steps and through the front entrance, followed by the dog. Marge couldn't fit her hat over her bun, so it sat precariously on top.

Chapter 2

The foyer was twice the size of Marge's living room, with its own fireplace and a wide staircase curving regally toward the second floor. Marge admired the newly hung wallpaper and ran her hand along the intricate wainscotting. She tilted her head back to look at the enormous chandelier that hung from a soaring ceiling.

"Close your mouth, Marge." Joey snickered.

"It's exquisite. I was quite unsuspecting of the mansion's grandeur."

Hugh led them through ornate double doors to the right.

Looking up as they passed through, Joey said, "These doors must be sixteen feet tall."

Marge looked up too, but then was distracted by Freida.

"Ooh. Imagine the party we could have in here." She spun around with her arms stretched wide, like a Disney princess. "A true ballroom. There's even a piano."

"Do you play?" Marge moved across the room and moved heavy draperies aside to see the view. Then wheezing and coughing, she made a face and backed away, brushing dust off her cerulean pantsuit.

"A little." Freida pressed several keys. "We'll need to have it tuned."

Only half listening to Freida's response, Marge pressed her nose against the window. "Behold, Joey!" He joined her there and she pointed out an overgrown but magical garden below the long, cement patio. "Visualize it blossoming and adorned with twinkle lights. It will be beguiling."

Hugh joined them, peering through the French doors. "I have a team of landscapers coming next week. The gardens are badly overgrown."

"My foot descended into a cavity in the forest. Have you observed them sprinkled about?"

"A cavity?"

"Holes," Joey said. "I've heard rumors about a treasure buried around here. Every few years the rumor is revived, and little groups of people come searching for it."

"You think they dig random holes around the property?" Hugh asked.

"Perhaps."

"I suppose that's as good an explanation as any other. Were you hurt, Ms. Bumfuzzle?"

"No, just slightly bruised."

⁘⟨⟩⁘

Leaving the ballroom and crossing the foyer, they entered the study to the left of the entrance. Hugh treated the room as a footnote on their way to the dining room, simply pointing out the fireplace, comfortable chairs, large desk, and bookshelves. A connecting door led into the formal dining room, which contained an elegant, twenty-person table and sideboard.

"All of the china and silver have been picked over or stolen by now," Hugh said, "but many of the larger pieces of furniture are still here."

"Most homes aren't big enough to hold them, I imagine," James said.

Freida trailed her fingers along the length of the table, making a face at the dust on her hand.

"Do you have any experience with carpentry?"

"Yes, a little. I worked as a handyman before I became a teamster."

Hugh nodded and lapsed into thought as he led the small group into the kitchen. All the rooms were enormous, but the kitchen took up a full corner of the ground floor.

A door passed from the dining room, and another from the foyer. The room, the same width as the dining room, continued around the corner of the house and behind the staircase.

The entire back wall was glass, leading into a greenhouse which could provide the household with herbs and vegetables. The greenhouse sat encircled by a walled-in garden, to protect it from weather and vandals. Two card tables and some folding chairs had been placed in the center of the kitchen, so the construction crew had a place to rest.

"You know," James said cautiously. "I don't want to talk myself out of a rental, but this place would make a great bed and breakfast."

"It might." Hugh nodded. "But it's a long time before that could happen. Why don't we rest for a moment? Would anyone like a bottle of water?" He opened a cooler and passed out water to everyone. "I was wondering, James, if you might be interested in living here rent free in exchange for doing some work, keeping it running and in good condition. I'll pay for any materials, of course, but perhaps you could gradually refinish the upstairs bedrooms— the wallpaper, bathroom tile, that kind of thing."

Hugh was smiling, and James was nodding. "What do you think, Freida?"

She stood and walked toward the glass wall of the greenhouse, smiling serenely. "The house is gorgeous. It might be fun to help with the transformation."

Hugh rose. "I'll let you think about it. Let's look at the last two rooms on this floor, then head upstairs."

<hr />

They exited the kitchen through an unobtrusive door behind the stairs that led back into the foyer and turned left toward the ballroom. Another set of tall, double doors led into the library.

"Where are the bathrooms?" James asked as they entered the library.

"Each bedroom has its own bath, which are being updated. Down here, small half baths are tucked into corners in each room, except the dining room. See that door over there?" Hugh pointed to a small door between bookshelves, before striding over and opening it. "This bathroom has a door on the other side that leads into the sitting room."

Joey admired the marble counter with double sinks and pointed out the linen closet before realizing that Marge was absent. He found her on a ladder in the library. "Marge? Are you sure that ladder is safe?"

"I didn't contemplate its safety." Her cerulean-clad backside reminded him of a clear summer sky, as she backed down to safety with a sneeze, and he thought her pants might go well with a sunny yellow blouse.

Before he could comment she said, "Observe this superfluity of books. Of approximated thousands, but a trickle appear to be absent." She sneezed again. "A plentitude of dust. What did I miss?"

"Hugh led us through a connecting bathroom to the sitting room. I'll show you." He rotated his walker and led Marge to the sitting room where the others were waiting.

As with the other rooms, most of the small furniture and decorative items had been removed, but a loveseat and matching sofa remained.

"You will notice that the fireplaces in each room are unique," Hugh said. "We've tried to restore everything to its original state and hope to obtain historical status for the house."

Joey examined the fireplace. "I wonder why no one stole the marble mantles," he whispered to Marge.

"Marble is weighty. Where does that door lead?"

Hugh opened the door and led them through. "This is a small, curtained alcove off the ballroom. It can be used as a place to store coats, or a small lounge if guests would like a rest."

They followed him through the ballroom and back into the foyer.

Joey eyed the grand staircase with trepidation.

Stopping at the base, Hugh said, "One of the first things the crew did was to repair and strengthen the stairs."

"James, could you carry my walker upstairs?"

"Sure." James took Joey's walker and returned it when they reached the landing. The horseshoe-shaped hall was open on three sides, looking over the foyer, a balustrade lining the outer edge for safety. Looking around, he said, "Have these banisters all been tested?"

"Yes, that was the second project, after the stairs." Hugh led them into the bedroom closest to the staircase. "These bedrooms are actually suites, with their own bathrooms and dressing rooms. The bedrooms on the third floor share bathrooms at each end of the hall." He opened heavy draperies to reveal a large, dusty, un-refurbished room.

"Seeing this room really highlights all the work that's been done downstairs," Joey commented.

Marge nodded as she eyed the cascading hundred-year-old wallpaper and dull wooden floors. A king-sized, four poster bed, covered with a dust cloth, sat prominently along one wall. The bed, another ornate fireplace, and a large, wooden armoire were all that survived, but ample space existed for a small table and chairs and a desk. The bathroom held a claw-foot tub, a toilet, and a marble counter, and another door led into a large changing room.

After viewing each room, Freida indicated that she liked the middle bedroom, boasting French doors which opened onto a large balcony.

"We'll work on this one first," Hugh told her. Leading them back downstairs, he continued, "The third floor is blocked off for now. We'll tackle that after we finish this floor. I've drawn up a contract for you to look over, if you're still interested in living here."

Hugh drew an envelope from his coat pocket and handed it to James. "Go ahead and read through it, discuss it, and make notes if there are any changes you want to make. Let's meet again on Monday."

"Great. Thank you very much." James shook his hand and turned to Joey. "Will you and Marge come too?"

"Of course. Just let us know when and where."

Chapter 3

Glancing around Millicent's living room, Marge thought it looked much like it did the day she moved in. With a layout similar to the other houses on Holly Lane, including Marge and Joey's, the sparse furniture and lack of knick-knacks gave it a very clean feel, and the combination of blue-green and white lent an ambiance of serenity. Her eyes lit on a painting propped in the corner about the same time her nose detected an aromatic smell wafting from the kitchen. "Something smells delicious. I trust you refrained from expending disproportionate effort."

"None of that. I love cooking for an audience. Come on through to the kitchen and have a seat. I made it in the crockpot and it's ready to eat." She placed heaping bowls of pot roast, potatoes, and carrots in front of Marge and Joey before dishing out her own. "I made bread too. Would you like some coffee?"

"Allow me to assist. You warrant a sojourn."

Millicent Beaumonde was in her seventies, small of stature, and pleasantly plump, but her posture and impeccable grooming lent her the air of someone much younger. She sat at the table while Marge poured them each a cup of coffee.

When Marge sat, she took a bite of beef and moaned quietly. "Millicent, this roast is melt-in-your-mouth delicious. I don't know how you create such delectables."

Millicent smiled with pleasure. "It's the fresh mint."

"Not merely the seasoning, it's positively succulent."

"The best I've ever had," Joey agreed.

"You two are making me blush." Millicent giggled. "Thank you, though. I'm glad you like it. I thought it would be good on such a cold day. Speaking of which, I'm thinking about moving back to the house on the hill for the winter."

"But you just moved in a few months ago." Joey popped another piece of roast in his mouth.

"I'm not going to move out, just stay with Elizabeth and the children for the winter. That way I won't have to worry about getting snowed in, losing electricity, not being able to get to the grocery store, that kind of thing."

"I do recognize the veracity of your reasoning, but we will feel your absence."

"I'll miss you too, but at my age, I just think it will be better."

"Incidentally, I adore that painting in the living room. Recherche. The child possesses an ethereal quality, almost as if she was a memory."

"The artist, Nicole Reid, is a local mystery. Her paintings are very popular, but no-one knows anything about her. I saw that one at the gallery in Chesterville and thought it would go perfectly with my furniture."

"A painting in that style would look stunning in Rutherford Mansion."

"Rutherford Mansion? That place has been vacant for decades."

"The new heir has been renovating and has agreed to rent it to James and Freida Nelson."

Millicent's eyebrows rose in surprise. "I was a number of years behind the Rutherford children in school. Even back then there were rumors of a curse."

"Do you know the story behind it?"

"Well, let me see." Millicent tipped her head, reminding Marge of a small bird. "The trouble seems to have started when Mr. Rutherford Senior, Abraham, had an affair with the caretaker's daughter. She was only in her teens and became pregnant. Refusing to acknowledge the child as his own, he fired the caretaker and gave him a reasonably large sum of money to disappear.

"The caretaker's wife, a mysterious lady, who some called a gypsy, walked through the woods to the newly constructed mansion.

No one in the family had ever heard her speak, but she stood at the front entrance and shouted with her fist in the air. 'A curse be on you, Abraham Rutherford. On you and this house and all of your lawful descendants. May unhappiness, sickness, and death claim every Rutherford who comes to live in this blighted place.'

"Those might not be the exact words, but they are a close approximation. I remember because they made quite an impression on me as a child."

Marge and Joey sat riveted.

"What subsequently transpired?" Marge asked.

"Mr. Rutherford laughed it off and told her to get off his land. The family left that night, never to be seen again, and that same night the kitchen caught on fire, leaving the scarred black stone."

"That might not have been the curse," Joey mused. "It might have been started by the caretaker."

"True, but since it was inside the house, there was some doubt. Anyway, the children had some unexplainable accidents before they were shipped off to boarding school, and their mother died in childbirth shortly after."

"What manner of accidents?" Marge had hardly touched her roast.

"A tree limb fell on Myrna and broke her leg. Bessie almost got hit by lightning. A large chandelier fell and killed one of the servants. Everyone said, 'Oh, what bad luck'."

"When did it stop?" Joey asked around a large bite.

"It didn't. When Abraham was on his deathbed, having suffered for years with tuberculosis, he called for his eldest daughter, Myrna. Shortly after she arrived, she ate poisonous mushrooms and died a week after he did. She left the house to her younger sister, who died in a car crash on her way to the funeral." Millicent shook her head. "The house next went to a young nephew of fifteen. He wasn't of legal age, so it sat vacant for six years. During that time, there were rumors of ghosts and at least one intruder was found dead, hanged from the banisters upstairs."

"I'm beginning to feel unwell," Marge said. "Such calamity."

"I didn't mean to ruin your lunch. I'm almost at the end of the story."

"Keep going. Pie will help us recover." Joey winked.

"She didn't mention pie."

"Well, the young man who inherited the house didn't believe in ghosts or curses, so on his twenty-first birthday, he held a giant Halloween party. He was cocky and full of bravado, drinking heavily and challenging his friends to daredevil antics.

"The next morning, his best friend and his fiancé were found dead in one of the guestrooms. The cause of death was unclear and there was some suspicion that the young heir—I'm sorry I can't remember his name—was responsible.

"He claimed it was the curse, and he closed up the house. It has been sitting empty and boarded up for decades."

"Now he has died, and Hugh has inherited." Joey sopped up the last of his gravy with a homemade dinner roll.

Marge was staring with wide eyes. "Do you think it's safe for Hugh to be renovating?"

"I suppose it would depend on whether you believe in curses or not. You're right; there has been so much tragedy. But if you look at each incident independently, they can be explained logically. Do you believe in curses?"

Taking a deep breath, Marge said, "I don't think so. Do you?"

"No, I don't."

"I don't either." Joey grinned lopsidedly. "Did you say something about pie?"

"I didn't, but you're in luck. I made a cherry pie this morning."

<hr>

After lunch, Marge helped Millicent with the dishes while Joey had a second piece of pie. They both thanked her for the wonderful lunch and the engrossing story.

"Let me know if anything else happens over there," Millicent said. "I can add it to the saga. I've been thinking about writing a history of our two families."

"That's a delightful notion, Millicent. I anticipate the historical society will be interested in sponsoring you." Marge hugged her. "Would you like us to stop for you on Sunday?"

"No, Elizabeth offered to pick me up, but thank you for asking."

Marge and Joey walked down the street in silence. Not an awkward silence, but rather the contented silence of two friends together with their individual thoughts. When they arrived in front of Marge's house, Joey said, "What do you want to do this evening? I'm feeling a little tired."

"Why don't we take our repose and reconvene for supper?"

"Sounds good. What time?"

"How about six? I'll throw something together."

"We should have asked Millicent for leftovers." He grinned.

"Would it be acceptable to dine at your house this evening?"

"Really?" When Marge nodded, he said, "I can just order takeout, so you don't have to carry everything over here."

Canting her head to the side, she thought that over. "Aren't you weary of restaurant food?"

"We've been pretty busy. I don't mind."

"That will simplify matters. You select your preference, and I will arrive at six."

He stood on the sidewalk in front of his house and watched her unlock her front door and brace herself for Fluster's cat-apult off the sofa. *See what I did there?* He snickered at his own joke. *I wonder what she's up to. Something for Christmas maybe.* He shrugged and went inside to have a rest.

Marge knew better than to lie down; she would sleep until six and wouldn't get anything done. She had much to do before the next day, so she rolled up her sleeves and started with the food preparation. At five-thirty she stopped what she was doing and took a quick shower. *We are going to have so much fun tomorrow.* She felt almost giddy.

Carrying a large canvas bag, Marge knocked on Joey's front door at exactly six o'clock and shivered. She didn't know what to expect because, as far as she knew, he didn't even have dishes. He took her coat and hung it up, then ushered her into the kitchen, where she stopped mid stride and gaped. Joey had set the table with fine china and silver cutlery, water and wine glasses, and cloth napkins. A bowl of salad sat in the middle of the table, with lit candles on either side.

"Have a seat," he said, pulling out a chair and pouring her a glass of wine.

Marge sat, placing her bag on the floor, and blinked at him. "I was unsure as to whether you possessed tableware."

Grinning, Joey sat down and poured himself a glass of wine. "I do have plates. They aren't rentals."

Marge laughed. "On what shall we dine this evening?"

"It's a surprise. Start with the salad."

When they were finished, he took the salad plates to the sink and said, "I might need some help with this next part. I don't want it to end up on the floor."

Marge joined him by the oven and looked inside. She breathed deeply to inhale the tantalizing aroma before accepting his offer of oven mitts and withdrawing a plate of fettuccine alfredo topped with grilled chicken. "This looks enticing and smells divine." She placed the plate atop the one on the table and went back for the second one. "Where did you obtain this elegant cuisine?"

"Would you believe me if I said I made it?"

"Did you?" she gasped.

"Taste it first, then I'll let you know."

"Watch your tie."

One shoulder slightly higher than the other, his bolo tie often hung askew, but it was more crooked than usual and in danger of joining the sauce-covered noodles resting on his plate. "Thanks. I might have ended up eating fettuccine a'la bolo." He chuckled.

They both agreed it was delicious. "I'm certain this is the most exceptional chicken alfredo I've ever eaten."

"Then I should admit that I didn't make it. There's a new caterer in town, and I hired him to cook our meal."

"I'm overwhelmed by all your effort. I was anticipating pizza."

"I got the impression that you wanted a home cooked meal, so I decided to give him a try."

"Delectable. We will unquestionably be equipped to endorse him after this."

When they had eaten all they could, Joey said, "I have one more surprise." He went to the refrigerator and withdrew a beautiful dish of chocolate mousse, turning to hand it to Marge. "Your dessert, mademoiselle."

She moved their plates aside and set it in front of Joey's chair, accepting another for herself. "I am astonished. This is the most wonderful meal I've had in a long time. It might possibly top Millicent's pot roast. Thank you so much."

"Honestly, I'm surprised too. I was hoping it would be good, but he exceeded my expectations."

<hr>

After dinner, Marge helped with the dishes, and they played several hands of cards before she excused herself. "I remain occupied at home but thank you again for the exquisite repast. It was worthy of formal wear."

"That's the joy of eating at home; you can wear whatever you want. Yoga tomorrow?"

"Yes, but not breakfast. I brought you two eggs, two pieces of bread, and a thermos of coffee to tide you over." She handed him the canvas bag and he chuckled. "I don't wish you to waste with hunger."

Chapter 4

Joey stood on Marge's front porch the next afternoon. He knew she was expecting him. She had, in her convoluted way, told him to bring his swimming trunks. He knocked again and rang the bell, but she still didn't answer, so he let himself in with his key. Whacking his walker lightly against the door frame and stomping the snow off his boots, he entered and hung his coat in the hall closet. He called out. "Marge. I'm here. Where are you?" The house was extremely warm, and he heard faint music coming from the kitchen, so he wandered in that direction, stopping in the entry to gape.

Marge was lying on a sun recliner in a bright orange bikini, an iced drink on a small table by her side and a vibrant pink umbrella over her head. Her eyes were covered by the round sunglasses perched on her nose, but her soft snore indicated she was asleep. Joey looked around in amazement, shaking his head at her rampant creativity.

The kitchen table had been pushed against the far wall and was covered in tropical-looking plants, which also strategically camouflaged the pantry and framed the French doors that led to the patio. A very bright sun lamp shone in one corner, and a light-weight carpet with a sand and surf pattern lay beneath the recliners. A beachball and a small plastic pool added to the atmosphere. The kitchen counter had been decorated to look like a tiki bar and a record player played reggae tunes. Marge had headed to the tropics without him.

"Marge?" He spoke softly so he wouldn't startle her, but she didn't wake. "Marge!"

She sat up abruptly and looked around before sinking back into her chair when she saw it was him.

"Put on your suit. The water's fine."

"How many cocktails have you had?"

"None, actually. This is iced tea." She picked up her glass and took a sip through the straw. "Now that you mention it, however, I could craft margaritas. I concocted Hawaiian-style teriyaki for supper. Where are you going?"

"I'm going to change into my trunks so I can enjoy our tropical vacation."

Marge smiled happily. "Shall I prepare margaritas?"

"Might as well."

When he rejoined Marge in the kitchen and took a seat on the second pool chair, she handed him a pink, frothy-looking frozen drink before resuming her seat. He noticed, once he was seated, that she had hung fairy lights around the kitchen. "You've gone to quite a lot of work. Do you plan on leaving it this way?"

"Yes, for an interval. Perhaps I should increase the flora. Do we have adequate color?"

"Do your swimsuit and the margaritas count?"

She canted her head to one side. "I believe so, but additional flowers would enhance our tropical vibe."

"Where are we going to eat?"

"I envisioned a picnic in the sand…or we could reposition the flora. It's not as enjoyable if you focus excessively on the particulars. The magic somehow dissipates."

"I was just curious. This is the most beautiful and amazing tropical paradise I've ever seen, and I'm very happy to be here sharing it with you." He held up his drink before taking a sip.

"You might desire sunscreen or an umbrella. The sun is quite intense."

"I'm not afraid of any old sunburn. Do you have any aloe?"

"I do."

"When's lunch?"

"At whatever time you desire.

"Fruit and sandwich triangles are available at the bar. Would you like me to retrieve some for you while I rotate the record?"

"You're the best. Thank you."

Marge turned the record over and put a plate on the small table between their chairs.

They ate their lunch and sipped their margaritas, then lounged in their recliners under the warm, artificial sun. Outside, the wind was howling, and the snow continued to fall, but Marge's cozy kitchen was a tropical dream.

"Should we get in the pool?" Marge asked after a while.

Joey eyed the wading pool. "It looks pretty small."

"We could alternate. Or we could play beach volleyball."

"What will we use for a net?"

"Is a net necessary? We could propel the beach ball hither and thither while preventing it from alighting on the sand."

"Right. And to make it interesting, we can sit in chairs across from each other with our feet in the water."

Marge laughed. "I'd better retrieve my towel in the event I am required to depart the pool precipitously."

"Is it okay to get the 'sand' wet?" Joey nodded at the carpet.

"We will have to cancel our picnic if the tide comes in." She arranged chairs on either side of the wading pool and set her towel on the floor near her feet, then waited for Joey to maneuver himself to the other chair. Once he was seated, she said, "Is grasping permitted, or only thwacking?"

"Let's start with a holding allowance and see how difficult it is, otherwise, you'll be up and down every turn."

"Excellent reasoning. Ready?"

"Yep."

Marge tossed the ball so lightly that it fell in the pool. "Drat. I didn't wish to launch it with excessive force."

Fetching it out of the pool, she tried again, and Joey caught it. As they played, they became more proficient and progressed to batting the ball back and forth without catching it.

Reaching high in the air and off to the side, Marge's rambunctious antics caused her chair to tip backward. Luckily, it bounced on her pool chair before landing on the floor, but looking up from her prone position she said, "Perhaps we should deviate from this pastime."

Joey chuckled. "What's next?"

"Hmm. Coconut bowling?"

"Do you actually have coconuts?"

"Certainly. I am prepared for almost any eventuality." She opened a children's indoor bowling set and took two coconuts out of the refrigerator.

"Where on earth did you get coconuts this time of year?"

"Do you recall what I said about the particulars? You may initiate our game."

They bowled for an hour, mostly because they were both terrible and laughed so hard their stomachs ached. Marge's coconut rolled under the table and Joey took out a plant. Fluster sat on the counter and scowled. They were debating a rematch when the lights flickered and went out.

Marge stood very still for a moment and blinked, then she switched on the battery-operated fairy lights. "I hope it doesn't become unseasonably cold at the beach."

"It's quite warm on this island but we could make a bonfire."

"A bonfire." Marge smiled with delight. "You build the fire while I set out our picnic."

⁂

Joey went into the living room and put his walker aside as he knelt by the fireplace. He noticed his joints felt better after staying in Marge's warm house all afternoon.

Winter was not a comfortable season for him, and he appreciated her efforts. Once the fire was crackling merrily, he returned to the kitchen where Marge had laid out a picnic blanket and plated two salads, along with teriyaki pork, white rice, and grilled pineapple. "This looks delicious, Marge." He joined her on the blanket and picked up a bottle of sesame salad dressing.

When the doorbell rang, Marge popped up and slid on a housecoat Joey hadn't noticed. "Be right back." She left the room and returned with their unofficially adopted nephew, Seth.

He was damp through, so Marge asked him if he'd like to put some of his clothes in the dryer. He looked around and said, "I'd rather eat. Something smells really good. Do you have any extra?"

"We have an abundance. I presume you will dry in due course. Here. Sit on this towel."

"What have you been up to, or should I even ask?"

Seth accepted a plate from Marge, then grinned at Joey. "We were in the park, making a snowman, when all the lights went out. Everywhere." He took a big bite of meat and closed his eyes. "So good. I want lots of this."

Joey waited patiently to hear the rest of the story.

"Sorry, Uncle Joey. The lights went out and someone threw a snowball, then suddenly we were all having a full-on snowball war. Carter jumped on me and smashed a snowball in my face, then I rolled over and put snow down his jacket and somehow it escalated."

Marge was staring at him with an incredulous look on her face, but Joey just grinned. "Don't worry, Marge. I imagine they were having a blast."

"We were. Can I have more meat?"

Marge gave him seconds and sat down again.

"While we were there, the last bus from Chesterville came in and a lady I've never seen got off the bus.

"It was really dark, even in the station so I was wondering if I should ask her if she needed help, but someone picked her up."

"Well, we do have visitors now and then. She might be here to visit relatives or something."

Seth shrugged and took another bite. "Carter said the car might belong to Mr. Stubbs, that real estate guy, then Peter came out to see what we were up to, and Carter's driver came to pick him up, so I decided to come over here."

"Are you staying over?" Joey asked.

"Yeah, if that's okay. My dad's working tonight."

"You're welcome any time."

"Can I go over there now and change my clothes?"

"Sure. I'll be back in a little while."

Seth took his plate to the sink, rinsed it, and put it in the dishwasher. "Thanks for dinner, Aunt Marge. It was the bomb."

"You're welcome, dear. See you tomorrow."

Joey stayed a while after Seth left. He helped Marge clean up their dishes, then poured them each a small glass of whiskey. They sat by the fire since the temperature had started to drop. Fluster sat on the back of the sofa and purred.

Chapter 5

After their morning yoga session, Marge descended to find Joey hard at work in the kitchen. He had not only made coffee and fed Fluster, but was in the process of making eggs, so she stuck some bread in the toaster, set the table, and poured them each a cup of coffee. "Where's Seth?"

"He wanted to sleep in." Joey plated the eggs and toast. "Enjoy your breakfast and then I have a surprise."

Marge grinned and clapped her hands. "I love surprises." She took a bite of the scrambled egg sandwich she had constructed. "You are becoming an exceptional chef. These are delicious."

It didn't take them long to eat and do the dishes, then leading her into the living room, Joey assisted Marge with her coat and opened the front door with a flourish.

"What is that?" she asked, pointing at an unusual vehicle parked at the curb.

"It's called a UTV. It's good for going off road and for driving on ice and snow. It even has an attachable snowplow and a winch for helping people out of drifts or ditches."

Walking slowly toward the strange little vehicle, Marge cocked her head and studied it. A gust of wind made her shiver, and her teeth began to chatter. The vehicle, with two seats in an enclosed cab and a small flat area in back for hauling, was painted in a green, camouflage pattern. "It looks like someone bred a miniature pickup truck with a dune buggy," she said finally.

"I bought the one with an enclosed cab and a heater, so we won't freeze in the wintertime. It's safer on ice than the car."

"Are we taking it to Rutherford Mansion?"

"Yes. The uneven ground is difficult with my walker. Maybe you can practice driving it, too."

25

Marge stepped back and looked at him out of the corner of her eye. "I'll just get my bag."

Joey climbed into the small cab and turned the heat up while he was waiting. The temperature had dropped even lower, and the wind blew frigid from the north.

When Marge returned, she was still shivering. "It's arduous to thaw once you get a chill. I'm grateful you selected the one with a heater."

Joey grinned. "Just wait until you see what this thing can do. It's amazing."

"When did you discover an opportunity for procurement?"

"I bought it online and had it delivered yesterday. It came while you were arranging your island paradise."

"You're sneaky," she teased.

"I know how you like to play in the snow, and we can use this for little errands too, like trips to the grocery store."

"I'm certainly relieved to have it at our disposal today. Another walk through the forest would be daunting."

"I'll admit, it's good timing."

They bounced along the dirt trail toward the milk plant and, cutting through the parking lot, turned left onto another dirt road, which came out of the forest to meet the paved driveway in front of Rutherford Mansion.

When Joey pulled into the drive at the front of the mansion, Freida came out to greet them.

Marge bounced out of the UTV and said, "What's our plan for today?"

"I have to finish packing."

"Are you in need of assistance?"

"I'm not sure yet. I'll be back for lunch, so I can let you know. James was asking for you earlier."

"We are available if you reconsider."

Finally locating James in the bedroom suite Freida had chosen, Marge gasped as they entered. "It's exquisite."

The newly finished wood floor gleamed. The wallpaper was cream colored with a pattern of small lilacs and the wainscotting matched the flowers in a light lavender. The mantle and trim around the fireplace were white, as were the windowsills. James led them through the room and into the dressing room, which had been transformed into a cedar-lined closet, with plenty of cubbies for shoes and hats.

After Marge had thoroughly admired the closet, James led them to the bathroom, which had been repainted and retiled. A clawfoot tub sat in one corner, and a modern, stone shower with a glass door sat opposite.

"Oh, James. Is this your design?"

"Yes, ma'am. Of course, it helps to know Freida's favorite colors and to have heard her daydreaming about what she'd like in her bathroom." He blushed slightly.

Marge grinned. "She must have been rapturous when she glimpsed the results of your labor."

"She did seem to like it." James blushed a little more.

Joey gave him a slap on the back. "It's a room worthy of your princess. You've even refinished the four-post bed frame."

"I haven't told Freida, but I ordered a new mattress to fit. The shop is delivering it tomorrow."

"You will need bedding in the correct dimensions. That shall be our housewarming gift," Marge said. "Is it king-sized or queen?"

"I think it's a king. I have the measurements here somewhere." He rummaged around in his pockets before pulling out a crumpled slip of paper and handing it to Marge. "Leave it to me to forget about something like sheets."

They went back downstairs to see how the rest of the house was progressing, and when James had left them to wander, Joey asked Marge when they would have time to pick out bedding.

"It has to be by tomorrow, right? Maybe we should make our excuses and drive into Chesterville."

Marge tilted her head. "I hadn't considered the timing. Perhaps you're right. Why don't you inform James and assure him we'll return promptly?"

Having made their excuses and returned to Joey's house, Marge waited on the curb for Joey to back his lovingly restored Model A out of the garage and replace it with his UTV. Marge, who didn't drive, enjoyed riding in his antique automobile because it made her feel like a celebrity. "Everyone stops and waves when we pass," she had told him on several occasions. He drove the thirty minutes to Chesterville, and parked near the entrance to the shopping mall, where he and Marge found a JC Penny.

Once inside, Joey stared at the rows of sheets and comforters in bewilderment. "How will we ever find what we're looking for?"

"We must establish the size of the bed, and luckily, we have James' measurements, then we choose the thread count, and select a color. I brought this." She pulled out a small piece of wainscotting, which had been cut after it was painted.

"Brilliant." Joey grinned.

After a preliminary search and asking a salesperson for assistance, they left the store with two sets of sheets and a comforter which had a cream and lavender pattern. "Freida may exchange the comforter if she has an alternate preference."

Joey was just glad to be done with it. Who knew picking out sheets could be so complicated? He put their purchases in the basket of his walker and wiped his forehead with a handkerchief.

Marge looked at her phone. "We will return with sufficient haste. Should we wrap our gift?"

"I don't think that's necessary. We can make the bed up when the mattress arrives."

"The sheets should be laundered."

"Why?"

She tilted her head and paused; her brow furrowed. "They usually are. I will activate the washing machine and provide Fluster his kibble when we stop to exchange vehicles."

Upon their return to the mansion, Freida was in tears and James sported a worried frown.

"Would you like to talk about it?" Marge asked her. "Why don't we get some coffee and sit by the fire?"

Freida burst into sobs again but followed Marge to the kitchen door.

Pouring her a cup and sitting across from her at the table, Marge waited patiently for Freida to tell her what had provoked her tears.

Finally, Freida looked at her and said, "It's my mother. She's decided to visit." Her lower lip trembled. "She's terrible, and she hates James. I moved here to get away from her."

Marge put her hand on Freida's and tilted her head, gazing at her young friend with compassion. "When will she arrive?"

"Tomorrow." Freida's shoulders slumped. "I told her we don't have a place for her to stay, but she said she's coming anyway."

"I expect she could lodge with me."

Freida's eyes widened in horror. "No. Marge, no. She… please don't even mention that. If she insists on coming, she'll have to stay at a hotel."

"Perhaps she wishes to apologize."

Shaking her head violently, Freida said, "She told me she's coming to talk me out of this madness. Her words. I've been so happy. I don't want her to come."

"And your father?"

"He's… he lives in town. They were never married, and they hate each other."

"Perhaps you could issue him an invitation as a potential distraction?"

Freida's eyes got a faraway look as she mulled that over. "I wonder."

"Who is your father? Is he an individual of my acquaintance?"

"His name is Mark Stubbs. He's a real estate agent."

"Why don't we ponder our options? Joey and I wish to invite you and James to the Fireside this evening. We can hearken to James and Joey's contemplations. Tomorrow is moving day."

Freida's eyes brightened. "Yes, I've been very excited about that. If only my mother didn't have such terrible timing." She frowned. "I wonder how she even knew."

Chapter 6

The little bell on the door signaled their arrival, and Helen looked up with a smile. "Good evening Ms. Bumfuzzle, Mr. Cattywampus. Sit wherever you like, and I'll be with you in a moment."

Heading for her favorite table, right in the center of the restaurant, Marge sat with Joey and closed her eyes, allowing the conversations around her to flow freely through her brain.

"I heard she's coming back."

"…construction at the Rutherford place."

"…saw a ghost at the milk plant."

"…stepping out on his wife."

"There'll be snow next week."

"…want to build a shopping mall."

James and Freida arrived at the table, and Marge opened her eyes and shook her head. Local gossip could be extremely accurate, or complete nonsense.

"Did you receive menus?"

"We probably don't need them." James glanced toward the cash register. "Here comes Helen."

Stopping at their table, Helen said, "The special today is steak and baked potatoes with a side of asparagus."

"I'll have that," Joey said, and was joined by a chorus of "me too."

"Four specials," Helen confirmed. "Anything to drink?"

Marge and Joey chose water, James asked for iced tea, and Freida ordered a rum and coke.

After Helen left, Freida said, "I asked my dad to meet us here. I hope you don't mind. Talking to him among friends seems less awkward."

"Will you inform him of your mother's impending arrival?"

"I don't think so. Otherwise, he might not show up."

James was silent, his face expressionless, but Marge noticed a tightness in his shoulders. *I hope I haven't given her bad advice. James doesn't seem to approve.*

They all looked toward the door when the small bell tinkled.

A slender man with a sharp, black goatee entered the Fireside and swiveled his head around, searching for someone. When his gaze landed on their table, he gave an almost imperceptible start, then smiled and walked toward them. "Freida, my girl. I was so glad to hear from you."

"Hello, Dad. Pull up a chair. We've just ordered. Have you eaten?"

"No." He looked nervously at Marge and Joey. "Who are your friends?"

Helen arrived with the drinks and took another order for the special and a Tom Collins.

After she left, Freida said, "These are friends of ours, Marge Bumfuzzle and Joey Cattywampus. They're helping us move into the Rutherford place."

Mark looked momentarily surprised, but recovered quickly and shook hands with Marge and Joey. "It's very nice to meet you." He shifted his attention to Freida.

"I thought maybe you'd like to come take a look at the place and maybe offer some advice, or even help out. And we'll be hosting a housewarming party in a couple of weeks, if you'd like to attend."

Marge glanced at James. This was the first she had heard of a housewarming party, but James remained stoic.

Smiling, Mark said, "Thank you, dear. It's very nice of you to include me. When would you like me to come?"

"We'll be moving in tomorrow, so you could come in the afternoon, if you like."

"Do you need help with moving?"

"No, I don't think so." She looked at James, who gave a subtle shake of his head. "We have everything packed and quite a few friends helping out."

Marge could almost see the wheels turning in Mark's head, trying to figure out what his daughter wanted. He will never guess.

Helen brought their food, and the rest of the meal was spent pleasantly talking about the house. Mark was surprisingly charming and appeared very interested in their plans.

"I'm quite excited to see what you've done with the place so far. I was told it was practically on the verge of being condemned and torn down."

"I don't know about that, but Hugh Rutherford has had a construction crew making the building safe, and it has passed all of the inspections so far," Joey said.

Mark paused, studying him. "Like I said, I can't wait to see it. What time shall I arrive?"

"Around noon? We usually take a little lunch break and can show you around," James said.

"Wonderful. I must get back to the office; I have a late appointment but thank you for inviting me to join you this evening, and I'll see you tomorrow. It was nice meeting you Ms. Bumfuzzle, Mr. Cattywampus." He walked to the register to settle his bill and gave them a little wave as he left the restaurant.

James' shoulders relaxed. "I hope you know what you're doing."

"Me too." Freida picked up her drink with a slender, shaky hand.

"Does he make you nervous?" Joey asked.

"Neither of my parents approve of our marriage, and my mom has told me things about my dad that sound shady. I don't know him very well." James took her hand in his enormous paw, and she leaned her fair head on his broad shoulder.

"He seems appreciative of his inclusion, and we will be present for moral support." Marge smiled.

"I think we'll head home if you don't mind." Freida looked wearily at Marge and Joey. "We have to get up early to start moving."

"At what time shall we arrive?"

"Whenever you like. We've arranged help unloading, and that will take some time. You can help me unpack when you get there if you don't mind."

When Helen returned to the table, she told them that Mr. Stubbs had paid for dinner, which caused some raised eyebrows.

"That was considerate," Marge said.

James gave a snort, and Freida frowned prettily. "See you tomorrow," he said. After helping Freida with her coat, he took her hand and headed for the door.

<hr>

Remaining at their table, Joey quietly observed Marge. She was sitting very still and looking at something invisible to everyone but her. "What is it, Marge?" he asked, finally, unable to bear the suspense.

She looked at him as if pulled from a dream. "Sorry?"

His eyes crinkled. "What are you puzzling over?"

"Did James and Freida date for an extensive period?"

"I'm not sure. Longer than I've known James. At least three or four years, I think. Why?"

"Freida doesn't appear to have had any interaction with her father in the recent past, but he and James are obviously acquainted and issued no greeting. I don't believe Mark was apprised of their connection with Rutherford Mansion, do you? If he was..." Marge paused and bit her lip.

"Are you ready to head home?"

"Yes, I suppose so."

Outside, the sun had set, and the air was very still. "How peculiar," Marge said.

"Let's not look a gift horse in the mouth. The walk home will be much nicer without that freezing wind."

Chapter 7

The moving truck had been unloaded and the furniture and boxes distributed to their allocated rooms by the time Marge and Joey arrived at Rutherford Mansion the next morning. Heading straight upstairs to see if the mattress had arrived, they found Freida in the bedroom, frowning at the bed.

"Marge! What do you have there?"

"A housewarming present from Joey and me. I hope it appeals to you." She laid the comforter and sheets on the bed. "I have laundered the sheets but deferred the removal of the tag on the comforter in the event you require an alternative."

"Oh, Marge!" Freida had tears in her eyes. "They're perfect. I was just wondering what I was going to do about bedding. You even have a flannel set. That will help with the cold." Freida hugged Marge fiercely, then hugged Joey too. "Thank you so much."

"Let me assist you with the appointment. You'll have an immaculate bed to sleep in tonight."

When they had finished, Freida stepped back to admire the finishing touch to her bedroom and smiled. "Will you help me unpack some clothes? Then we can go work on the kitchen." She turned to Marge and laughed.

Marge was already opening boxes and shuttling the linens to Joey, who had begun to place them in the spacious bathroom cupboards. Freida had packed and labelled each dresser drawer and hung items from the closet in a wardrobe box, so they quickly restored everything to its appropriate place. Marge, glancing around the room, noticed a desk bearing a laptop near the window.

"I work from home, but I took this week off."

"I am discomfited by my assumption that you were unemployed."

"I have a very flexible schedule, so people might think so."

"What is your occupation?"

Dainty bracelets clinked together as Freida ran a hand through her straight brown hair. "I do freelance editing and copywriting, and I'm writing a book." Her soft, brown eyes lit up. "It's slow going because I've been very busy, but it's coming along."

"That's wonderful. Can you chronicle the storyline?"

"It's a fantasy novel about fairies who take care of people who get lost or injured in the woods and struggle to defend their home against those trying to destroy it."

"I would be delighted to read it when it is completed," Marge said kindly. "Shall we proceed to the kitchen?"

"Almost, but I wonder if you could help me with one more thing. We decided to wait to unpack most of the books and decorative items, and the boxes are stacked in the spare rooms. One box has some of my supplies in it, and I'll need them when I start working again. Could you help me find it? It's labeled 'office' I think."

"Certainly, dear." Marge glanced at Joey. "How are you progressing?"

"I'm almost done. I'll wait for you here."

Marge and Freida peeked into several unfinished rooms before they found a stack of boxes in the final room at the end of the hall. The room was dark, so Marge opened the heavy draperies as Freida began shifting boxes. When she turned from the window, a shaft of sunlight hit a beautiful, dust-covered painting. Something about it stirred a memory, so she walked closer and set it on an antique dressing table. "Freida, have you noticed this painting?" Marge continued studying the tranquil blue and green hues, and the otherworldly image of a happy child running through a field.

Freida approached and made an 'oh' with her mouth. "That's gorgeous. We should hang it downstairs in the foyer."

"Yes, exquisite." Marge continued to pick at the memory the painting invoked as she helped Freida find her office supplies.

After the box was finally unearthed and carried to Freida's bedroom, they returned for the painting. It was unwieldy due to its size, so they each took an end and carried it to Freida's bedroom as well.

The artists' signature was on Marge's end, and she almost dropped the painting when she saw it. "Nicole Reid," she breathed. "Identical to the painting in Millicent's living room."

"Are you okay, Marge?"

"Yes. I was merely astonished by the artists' signature. How did this painting come to reside here?"

Leaning it against her bed, Freida shrugged. "Who knows? It's pretty dusty, so it must have been here for a while."

"Joey, observe this painting," Marge called.

He was wiping the painting's dust off with his handkerchief when James' voice boomed up the stairs. "Freida. Your dad is here."

Heading out of Freida's room and looking over the balustrade, Joey gaped. "Who's that with him?" Freida asked.

"Sayuri," Joey said in a strangled voice.

Marge leaned forward and spoke in his ear. "Your former spouse?"

He nodded, then gave himself a shake. "She's the last person I expected to see."

Freida looked from one to the other and said, "I'll take them into the kitchen. Thank you both so much. Are you hungry?"

"I'm always hungry," Joey mumbled, and Freida bounced down the stairs. "Hi, Dad," he heard her call. "Come on through to the kitchen."

Marge wasn't sure what to say, so she opted for a practical response. "Allow me to convey your walker."

Joey handed it to her and grabbed the railing, slowly making his way downstairs.

Marge returned his walker when they reached the foyer and followed him to the kitchen.

James was shifting boxes from the wooden, rectangular table and had offered chairs to Mark and Sayuri. Freida was pouring coffee for everyone. "So, Dad, who's your friend?"

"This is Sayuri," he said with a smile.

"Hello, Joey."

Her shiny black bob and dark eyes were in sharp contrast to her pale skin, and Marge thought her very beautiful.

Joey didn't answer immediately, but the awkward moment dissolved when Dog bounded into the kitchen. Sayuri was still looking at Joey but everyone else's attention, except Marge's, was on the four-legged, tail-wagging, attention-seeker.

After he had visited everyone around the table, Dog sat next to Freida and put his head in her lap. "I love him so much. I've always wanted a dog. We need to come up with a name for him." She stroked his ears. "I thought we should name him Happy, but James said we should call him something that sounds like Dog, so he knows that's his name. What do you think?"

"What might resonate with Dog?" Marge asked.

"Paws," Joey said.

"That's an excellent suggestion. Come here, Paws," Marge called, and although he didn't move from Freida's side, he did look up and thump his tail.

"Dr. Harkins will be stopping by this afternoon to give him a checkup, and we can give him a flea bath," James said.

"He does some strange things, sometimes." Freida continued stroking his ears. "Like he'll suddenly stare at the wall and whine. I hope we don't have a ghost." Freida shivered.

"He's probably staring at a bug." James put his arm around her shoulders and placed a kiss on her temple. "What brings you to Buckwood, Sayuri?"

Sayuri looked at Mark.

"She's married to my business partner." The doorbell rang, and Mark stood instantly. "I'll get that," he said, before rushing out of the kitchen.

Chapter 8

Curious, James followed Mark as he raced from the room. Mark flung open the door and froze. Dressed in a business suit, with her pale blonde hair carefully pinned into a smooth French twist, Freida's mother gazed at him, expressionless.

"Caroline."

"Oh, no," thought James, as he approached them.

"What are you doing here?" Caroline said coldly.

"I'm visiting our daughter."

Eying him with distaste, she shifted her focus. "James."

"Welcome, Caroline."

"Do you have my room ready?"

James' eyes widened in surprise. "Didn't Freida tell you that we don't have a spare room yet?"

"She did but look at the size of this place. I suppose *he's* staying here." She nodded toward Mark, her expression full of loathing.

Freida had entered the foyer to see what was going on. She trembled when she saw her mother in the entryway, and James took her hand.

"What is the meaning of this, Freida?" Caroline's voice shook with anger.

"I have as much right to be here as you do."

"You gave up your rights long ago. Freida, I demand an explanation."

Freida, with a look of complete innocence, said, "Dad has been a huge help with the move."

"Don't call him that. Is he staying here?"

"No, mother. I told you, only one room has been completed."

"Then, I can stay in that one."

"No, that is *our* room."

"Or you could come stay with me." Mark winked at her.

"Over my dead body. If you don't want me here, Freida, I will just go to a hotel."

Freida remained silent.

"You are a terrible, ungrateful excuse for a daughter. Call me a taxi."

"I'll give you a ride." Mark smirked.

Caroline turned her back on him and grabbed the handle of her suitcase.

"Mom? Why don't you join us in the kitchen for a cup of coffee while you wait? And maybe a sandwich?"

"I don't want coffee. Or sandwiches. I'm so disappointed in you, Freida. You can come have a meal with me at the hotel when you don't have company." She slammed the front door and rolled her suitcase to the circular drive, where she gingerly perched on the edge of it to wait.

"Is this why you invited me here?" Mark asked.

"Partly. I'm sorry, Dad."

"It was a mean trick, but I forgive you." He smiled.

"I heard so many terrible things growing up that I thought you were a monster. Was any of it true?"

"I don't know what you heard, but probably not. Your mother's very ambitious and left me for someone higher up the ladder. I have no idea why she hates me so much, but I'm glad you and I got a second chance."

"Me too, Dad." Freida hugged him and called for a taxi.

James, who didn't like either of Freida's parents and had difficulty understanding their family dynamic, silently accompanied them back into the kitchen.

Marge, Joey, and Sayuri were sitting in silence, the tension almost palpable.

"Why don't I take you and Sayuri on a little tour while we wait for lunch?" James asked.

"Great idea," Mark said. "Come on, Sayuri."

She glanced at Joey before rising and following James and Mark out of the kitchen.

"Thank goodness for James." Freida poured herself another cup of coffee. "Would either of you like another cup?"

"I can pour, and start another pot," Marge offered. "You should take a little break."

—————————⚬⚬⚬—————————

The doorbell rang a second time, and James returned from his tour with a bag of sandwiches.

When Mark was seated, he said, "The house looks amazing, but isn't it a little big for just the two of you?"

Freida fidgeted. "We're talking with Hugh about opening a bed and breakfast once the renovations are finished."

"That's a great idea," Mark said, after a little pause. "I have a client who was interested in purchasing this place, but after all of the work that's already been put into it, I don't think the price would be right."

"Hugh Rutherford has put in an application for historical status, too, so no one will be able to tear it down. He wants to keep it in the family," James said firmly.

"Well, since this project is a go, how can I help?"

"How are you at moving furniture around?

Walking to the door, James turned and said, "I imagine you ladies will be working on the kitchen."

"Yes." Freida grinned. "We want to keep you fed."

James winked at her and left the room with Mark and Joey in tow.

"Let's get you unpacked," Marge said as the men left the room.

"I bought some things for Paws, too. I have them here." Freida pulled out a box that was larger than the others.

"Sayuri, we weren't introduced, but I'm Marge."

Sayuri smiled. "Hi Marge. I'm Joey's ex-wife."

"Yes, I know," Marge said quietly. "Do you wish to assist with the unpacking?"

"I'll just watch if you don't mind. I don't want to break a nail."

Marge glanced at her perfect manicure and nodded, then she turned to Freida and said, "The kitchen is dazzling. I adore the color scheme."

"I love it too. James did the painting when I wasn't looking." They both stood and took in the gleaming white tile, offset by the lavender table and matching cupboards.

"Let's empty these boxes so we can properly admire his work. Behold, harmonizing curtains." Marge searched through the boxes for the most important, everyday dishes, while Freida looked in the refrigerator.

"We'll have to stock up on food."

"Have you determined the placement of your kitchenware?"

Freida walked around, looking in cabinets and moving boxes. "The glasses and mugs here, near the sink, and the plates in the next one over, do you think?"

Marge nodded and opened one of the boxes of glasses.

"Then, the pots and pans over here by the stove." Shifting two more boxes she said, "Let's start with that and then figure it out as we go."

Sayuri sat and watched for a few minutes, then quietly slipped out of the kitchen.

⚬

They heard the thump of Joey's walker before he entered. He glanced around the beautiful room. "Where did all the boxes go?"

Freida laughed. "Marge is a powerhouse. We're just about finished."

"Why don't you two take a little break?"

"I fear if I take a seat, I might be unable to rise."

Marge pushed a long strand of curly, orange hair off her damp forehead with a dust-covered finger, leaving a streak of dirt.

"Let's take a break. I'm sorry, Marge. I can't thank you enough. You've been working so hard."

"As have you. It's gratifying to witness everything in its place."

"Is my dad still here?" Freida asked Joey.

"I think he was just leaving. He's been a very big help."

"I wondered."

Joey studied Marge's face. "How are you holding up?"

"I will sleep well tonight. I yearn for a jacuzzi."

"Maybe we should install one on your back porch."

"Tonight?" She laughed. "A bath may be adequate."

<hr>

When Dr. Harkins arrived, Freida went searching for Paws.

After giving the wiggly Golden Retriever a thorough checkup, he said, "Paws appears to be in perfect health. Would you like a hand cleaning him up?" He finished clipping Paws' nails and swabbed out his ears.

"Yes, please," Freida said. "I've never had a dog before, and I'm not sure how to go about giving him a flea bath. I asked James to light the fire in the sitting room, so he'll have a warm place to dry off. I hope he won't mind being a house dog."

"There's plenty of room to run around, and as long as you give him food and attention, I imagine he'll be very happy." The vet smiled at her. "Do you have a hose? That would be less messy than a bathtub. And some towels. I hope you don't mind getting wet."

Once they had unearthed all the necessary supplies, they put a harness on Paws and set about giving him a bath. They chose the patio so he wouldn't roll in the mud, and he was enchanted with this new game, wiggling around and trying to drink from the hose.

They were all thoroughly soaked in the end, but Paws was clean and flea-free.

They dried him and themselves as best they could, and the vet put a new flea collar around his neck. Leading him to his new bed in front of the fireplace, Freida let him settle in before rewarding him with a rawhide bone.

James entered the sitting room and chuckled. "It looks like all of you got a bath."

"We'll need to change. How long before we wrap things up today?"

"Not much longer. Marge can stay in here by the fire and keep an eye on Paws."

Marge watched the two of them leave the room, then turned her attention back to Paws. He had curled up with his bone and was fast asleep. The heat from the fire was making her sleepy too, but she didn't want to sit on the newly upholstered chairs when she was wet. She had begun swaying on her feet by the time Joey found her.

"Are you ready to go home?"

"Yes, I am desirous of dry clothing. How about you?"

He nodded. "We can come back tomorrow if you like."

Chapter 9

The shrill sound of the telephone roused Marge from a deep sleep. She glanced at her bedside clock and saw that it was one o'clock. *One o'clock? How can that be? Did I sleep right through dinner? Poor Joey.* The telephone stopped ringing, then began again.

Sitting up, Marge rubbed the sleep from her eyes and picked up the receiver. "Hello? It's okay. Yes, come right over. I'll be down in a minute." She replaced the receiver and went into the bathroom to splash some water on her face before descending the stairs to let Joey in.

"Have you eaten?" She asked when she answered the door.

"A long time ago. I ordered a pizza." He handed her a box from the walker's basket. "We can have some while I tell you why I'm here in the middle of the night."

"I was counting the hours, and I've already had a full night's sleep. Cold or hot?" she asked, referring to the pizza.

"Cold, of course. We could reheat the coffee from yesterday."

Marge stuck two mugs of coffee in the microwave and set the pizza box and two plates on the table. "So, what has transpired? Did you have a nightmare?"

"Yes, but that's not why I'm here."

Marge had been having a nightmare, too. She dreamt that Sayuri convinced Joey to remarry her and move away from Buckwood. She was grateful for the telephone call.

"Right before I called you, James called. Freida is in hysterics, and he needs us to go over to the mansion to help out. She said she saw a ghost," Joey continued.

"Should we not make haste?"

"Yes, but eat something first. We might be a while and you didn't have dinner."

Marge was already eating. She finished chewing a bite and asked, "Did James provide any details?"

"No, he just asked if we would come."

"We could take the pizza with us." She took another bite.

"We'll probably be busy when we get there, so eat another piece, then put on your ninja duds and we'll go."

When Joey pulled up in front of Rutherford Mansion, all the downstairs lights were on. He rang the bell and shivered in the cold, early morning air. Answering almost immediately, James led him and Marge across the foyer into the sitting room where Freida sat huddled in a blanket, staring at the brightly burning logs in the fireplace. She looked up with frightened eyes when Marge and Joey entered the room.

Marge walked over and sat next to her, taking her hand. "Why don't you recount what occurred?" she asked gently.

"I w-went into the k-kitchen for a glass of w-water and I s-saw a g-ghost." Freida shivered violently.

"What convinced you it was a ghost?"

"S-she was all w-white, even her hair, and s-she disappeared into a w-wall."

James' face was pinched with worry.

"Will you show me where you saw her?" Marge asked gently.

Freida nodded and stood, but she didn't let go of Marge's hand. Paws, who had been lying in front of the fire, raised his head. He got up and joined Freida as she walked toward the kitchen, her steps slowing as she got closer.

"Did you activate the illumination?"

"No, t-the moonlight was s-shining through the g-greenhouse glass, so I c-could see where I was going. She was glowing."

Marge could feel her tremble beneath the strong grip of her hand. "Where were you positioned when you observed the apparition?"

"Ab-bout here." Freida stopped halfway between the door and the kitchen table and pointed toward the sink. "She was over there."

"What was she doing?"

"It looked like she was getting a glass of water." Freida's eyebrows drew together as she thought back.

"Did she observe your presence?"

"I d-don't think so."

"And what ensued?"

"She w-walked around that corner and disappeared."

"We are unable to see around the corner from this position. Did you pursue her?"

"Yes, but when I turned the corner, she was g-gone." Freida's eyes appeared very large and she trembled.

Still holding her hand, Marge walked over to the sink, then across the kitchen. At the end of the room, hidden by the pantry, was a short, L-shaped hallway that led to the laundry room. There was no exit at that end of the room, nowhere for anyone to escape, other than a small window, which was included in the recently installed alarm system.

Paws sat and stared at the wall with a soft whine.

Freida shuddered. "There have been other things."

"What do you mean?"

"I have places where I keep things, little baskets and hooks. Things that I put away yesterday afternoon and last night are not where I left them. Curtains that were drawn have been opened. Area rugs and pictures have been moved. James and I walked through the house, checking everything."

Freida continued to cling to Marge's hand as Marge approached Paws. She ran her hand along the wall, then canted her head. They walked from one end of the wall to the other, Marge knocking on the wall in random locations, then reversing direction, knocking again.

"Hmm. Let us return to the sitting room."

James and Joey were sitting in front of the fire when the ladies returned. "I am unconvinced Freida observed a ghost," Marge said.

"But I did!"

"What variety of ghost imbibes tap water?"

"I thought you would believe me."

"I do not mean to infer that you did not observe an entity, however…"

"Someone wants you to think there's a ghost," Joey said quietly. "Has it occurred to you that not having a ghost might be worse?"

"Yes."

Freida looked at James sharply.

"I know you're afraid of ghosts, honey, but if it's not a ghost, someone has access to our home, and we don't know who that person is."

Still speaking quietly, Joey said, "My suggestion is that you two turn off all the lights and make a production of going back to bed. You can talk about how Marge and I are going to sleep in the sitting room, but keep an eye out in your bedroom, and we'll stake out the kitchen and the foyer to see if we can catch the intruder in the act. Even if it's a ghost, Freida said it's visible, so we'll see it if it appears. This morning's objective is not to apprehend the person or ghost, just to see what they're up to and hopefully how they are coming and going. This might take a day or two because if it's not a ghost, they have to sleep sometime."

"What about you? You need to sleep." Freida said.

"We already had a full-night's sleep," Marge said. "At least, I did." She looked at Joey.

"I had plenty of sleep as well. We'll be fine."

"Alright then." James took Freida's hand and grinned. "Let's get to bed, little lady."

She giggled despite herself and followed him up the stairs.

Marge helped Joey quietly situate himself at the kitchen table, and she grabbed a piece of pizza and a glass of water before placing a folding chair beneath the staircase. They decided to text if they saw anything or needed a change of scenery or a bathroom break and let Paws roam freely.

After a couple of hours, Marge grew restless. She was about to visit Joey in the kitchen when she caught movement from the corner of her eye. A bulky figure emerged from the study, stopped near the doorway, and scanned the foyer. The moonlight from the large front windows cast a shadow against the figure's dark-clad frame, but Marge was invisible to the person, sitting quietly in the darkened alcove beneath the staircase.

The intruder silently crossed the foyer and removed the Nicole Reid painting from the wall where it had been hung, before backing slowly toward the study, spinning around, and reentering the room. After the person entered the study, Marge texted Joey and told him to come as quickly as he could.

Together they approached the study and peeked inside. The room was empty. Joey heard her string of stinkers as he pointed at the door to the dining room before making his way back to the kitchen. Marge approached the door and met Joey in the doorway between the dining room and the kitchen.

"Darn," he whispered. "Who was it?"

"I could not discern his identity. He appropriated the painting Freida and I discovered upstairs."

"He must have gone through the kitchen when I left. Are you sure it was a man?"

"No, I did not assert the intruder was male. He seemed big and bulky, but he or she might have been wearing a thick coat."

"The multiple doors present a problem. Come and have some more pizza. It's going to be light outside pretty soon, so I don't imagine our 'ghost' will be back until tonight. I wonder why he took that painting."

"I am unable to profess a motive. It's lovely, but still…" Marge opened the pizza box and took out a slice of cold pepperoni.

"Are you up for another stakeout tonight?"

"Yes, but a nap is required if we are going to repeatedly maintain our late-night vigil."

They were formulating a plan when James entered the kitchen at six looking tired, his face haggard.

"You're up early," Joey commented.

"I have work this morning. Did anything happen?"

"Yes, someone stole that painting you hung in the foyer, but he or she disappeared again. We'll keep watch again tonight."

"I feel bad keeping you up all night."

"We will take our repose during daylight hours," Marge said around bites. "You can't perform a stakeout alone, and you have Freida and work to consider. We can sleep after she rises. Is she safe upstairs by herself?"

"She was sleeping so soundly I didn't want to wake her, so I left Paws with her."

"What time does she ordinarily wake?"

"Seven or eight, but she was awake for hours last night, so I'm not sure what time she might wake up this morning."

"I'll keep an ear out," Marge said. "We won't depart before she's awake and the construction crew has arrived."

"Thank you both. I don't know how I can ever repay you."

"We're your friends. You don't need to worry about that."

"I feel very lucky. I don't know if I could leave Freida to go to work if you weren't here. I don't like to frighten her, but this business with the intruder has me very worried."

"It's definitely something to be taken seriously," Joey said. "We'll take care of her while you're gone."

"Shouldn't we call the police?" Marge asked.

"What would we say? We might have a ghost?"

"We'll try to figure out how they are gaining access to the house, then we'll call the police," Joey said.

James finished his coffee, thanked them again, and left for work.

At seven, Marge heard Freida scream, "James? James, where are you?"

Paws nearly knocked her down as she sprinted up the stairs. Arriving at Freida's bedroom door, out of breath, she bent with her hands on her knees.

"James is gone!"

"He went to work, dear. Joey and I are here."

Freida swiped away her tears and gave Marge a rueful smile. "I should have remembered that. I thought the ghost got him."

"I don't really think you've got a ghost, dear."

She told Freida about the intruder who stole the painting.

"But that might be worse. Some stranger has been wandering through my room, moving things around. What if he's a murderer?" Her voice rose higher as she spoke, finally ending in a squeak.

"Joey and I will stay up again tonight and try to catch him."

"I don't want you to get hurt. What if he's dangerous?" She stopped and stared at Marge. "Wait a minute. The ghost I saw was a woman. What if we have a ghost *and* a murderer?"

"There might be two people involved, but what manner of ghosts would be drinking glasses of water from the tap and physically conveying giant paintings through the house?"

Freida canted her head and scrunched up her nose. "It would be more ghostly if the glass or painting was levitating."

"Regardless, we won't confront them. We will merely attempt to discover their access point, then we can inform the police. Now, you should get dressed. What time do the workers arrive?"

She was answered by the sound of hammering. "They get here early. It's so exciting seeing the house transform. I'll get dressed and meet you downstairs. Where is Paws?"

"He's waiting in the hall."
"I'd like him to stay with me."

Chapter 10

Marge returned downstairs to find Joey making coffee and chatting with Hugh. They waited until Freida descended, then made their excuses and promised to return that evening.

"It's already ten, so if we want to get back here before it's too late, we should try to get some sleep now."

"I believe I could sleep." Marge yawned. "We'll have to determine what to do about dinner, too."

"Set your alarm for eight or nine hours, and I'll bring food."

"Splendid. Will you be able to sleep?"

"Yes. I might take a hot bath first."

"I missed mine yesterday. A hot bath and a small glass of whiskey sounds pleasant."

Chuckling, Joey shook his head as he pulled up in front of her house. "Don't fall asleep in there. You won't be happy when you wake in cold water."

Marge laughed, too, and after bidding him adieu, got out of the UTV and rushed to open her front door. Fluster flung himself at her as soon as she entered and meowed long and loud about his upset schedule.

"I'm sorry, Fluster. My poor baby. Are you hungry?"

He jumped down and stalked to the kitchen, waiting by his bowl, just in case she didn't understand.

Feeding him first, she then turned up the thermostat and went upstairs to draw her bath. Returning downstairs to pour herself a small drink, she took a minute to brush her feline friend. *He's lonely. I wish I could take him with me, but Paws would frighten him.*

After brushing him, Marge turned out the lights and took her drink upstairs to enjoy with her bath.

❦

Joey hadn't slept much the previous day and knew he was tired enough to easily sleep, despite the odd hour. He woke to nightmares twice but managed to sleep in between. The second one, however, had him fully awake and sweating profusely so he decided to stay up. *It's six anyway. I'll order food. I wonder what Marge would like.*

He dressed in all black and studied his list of take-out restaurants, finally deciding on submarine sandwiches. *That way we can snack if we get hungry or bored.* He ordered five kinds, cut in thirds, and was told to expect them in half an hour.

At seven o'clock, always the optimist, Joey arrived on Marge's doorstep with a large package of sandwiches. He noted the lack of light coming from the house and knocked loudly. He waited a few moments before knocking again and he shivered. Even with an extra layer of long underwear, the wind cut through everything. Finally, he rang the doorbell and was answered by the appearance of a light inside.

Marge, her curly, waist-long hair flowing wildly in all directions, rubbed the sleep from her eyes and smiled. "I even set my alarm this time, but I slept right through it. I must have been exhausted."

"I suspect you were."

"What do you have there?"

"I got submarine sandwiches so we can snack later."

"Excellent. I will commence brewing, and we shall bear thermoses. It's going to be a prolonged evening. Last night we didn't initiate our stakeout until two."

"Would you like me to braid your hair so you can wear a cap like you did at the milk plant?"

Marge clapped her hands.

"That will be a pleasure. I will change after we dine and convey my brush. I'm famished."

"Me too, so I ordered a lot. Plus, we might have to share if James sees them." Joey chuckled.

After they ate and Marge was dressed in black polyester, her hair braided down her back compliments of Joey, she fed Fluster again to make sure he had food while she was absent and declared herself ready.

"Did you say something about thermoses?"

"Oh, yes, I did." She pulled two from the cupboard and filled them, then carried them out to the front hall.

There weren't as many lights on as the night before, and when James opened the door, he escorted them into the sitting room where Freida was again resting before the fireplace. She looked much calmer and smiled when they entered. "I was wondering when you'd get here."

"How did you fare today?" Marge asked, perching beside her on the loveseat.

"It went well, and James got home at three, so we had a nice dinner together. Thank you again for coming. You promise not to confront the intruders, right?"

"We promise," Joey said.

They chatted for another hour, then James and Freida said goodnight and headed upstairs. After they left, Joey said, "We should probably assume that our 'ghosts' know we're here again, because the UTV is parked out front, but that didn't stop the person who took the painting. Perhaps once the house is dark and the sitting room door is closed, they'll think we've gone to bed."

"That's a fair assumption. Shall we proceed as we did last night?"

"We can. I also put cloth covers on my walker, so it doesn't make so much noise on the wooden floors. We can probably hang out for a while, using the lights, then pretend to go to sleep. Want to play some cards? Or have another snack?"

"Yes, and yes, and we should use the facilities before the stakeout officially begins. Where is Paws? Did he go upstairs?"

"I think so. He follows Freida everywhere."

They played several rousing hands of Go Fish and snacked on sandwiches, then at eleven o'clock, Joey put the sandwiches in the refrigerator and turned out all the kitchen lights, remaining seated at the table. Marge went into the sitting room, turned out the light, and shut the door behind her when she left to take up her post behind the stairs.

Chapter 11

The shadows from the moonlight drew Marge's attention to the odd dimensions of the rooms, particularly those of the study. She quietly entered and left the room, noting the angle of the wall in the foyer and that of the wall inside the room. The inside wall, lined with bookshelves, seemed to angle inward, making the room narrower on one side. Placing the flashlight in the pocket of her coat, since it was quite chilly in the darkened room, she set her phone on one of the shelves and started pulling out books.

She was about to give up and move to another room, when she found several books stuck together on the shelves. Attempting to pull them out, the bookshelf swung toward her, leaving a dark, narrow entrance behind it. Marge turned on her flashlight and peered inside. She thought about calling Joey, but the passage was too narrow for his walker and small, enclosed spaces were one of his triggers.

Standing at the entrance, she debated the wisdom of entering until her curiosity finally got the better of her, compelling her to enter the passage and find out where it led.

Marge carefully took one step inside, and then another, a frisson of fear snaking up her spine as the bookshelf slowly swung back into place. Standing very still in the dank, inky darkness, Marge used every one of her senses.

Made entirely of stone, the absence of light in the passage seemed to absorb the beam from her flashlight. She was unable to see more than a few feet in front of her, but she could feel the hard stones through her boots, and her left hand felt the damp chill of the wall. She heard dripping and the sound of her own breathing. She registered the smell of damp earth and then wrinkled her nose as she also smelled her string of stinkers that had no escape.

57

Time became indefinable as she slowly made her way through the passage. Splitting at intervals, stone steps led up and down, and although Marge attempted to keep her bearings, she became hopelessly turned around.

Stumbling as she descended a particularly rough set of steps, she dropped her flashlight. Engulfed in a black void, the air once again filled with the sound and fury of her nervous flatulence, and her small gasp of despair. An intense feeling of claustrophobia assailed her, and she thought at once of Joey.

"I can do this," she said aloud. The sound echoed around her. *I hope I don't have company*. She closed her eyes and took several deep breaths. I can do it.

When she opened her eyes, the passage remained pitch black, providing no clue as to which direction she should take, other than the way she was facing. Slowly walking forward with only her hands and feet to guide her, Marge continued.

I'm getting the hang of this, but how will I ever exit?

Her foot met air, and she pressed her hands against the wall and bent her knees to sit, her heart pounding. Her bottom hit the stone floor and bounced off the top stair before her feet found purchase, stopping her fall. She sat panting, afraid to move.

Closing her eyes she prayed, "Lord, please don't let me die in here. Give me strength and courage and guide me with your light. I don't think I can do it on my own."

A sense of calm enveloped her as she continued to sit with her eyes closed until her heartbeat returned to normal. Finally, she turned so she was on her hands and knees and crawled up the top step to the flat surface she had been walking on, then, using the walls, she rose to her feet.

She stood quietly. Whenever I found stairs before, one went up and another went down. *I came from that direction, so there must be another, but my hands didn't feel anything… Maybe I'm at the top. Is there an exit here?*

She felt around the walls on either side of the passage with her fingers and accidentally triggered a door that led into the back of a small storage room. She was trembling and close to tears when she collapsed into the room, and the secret door began to close behind her.

Marge lay on the ground for a few minutes, allowing herself to rest and decompress. "Thank you, Lord," she whispered.

Further exploration wasn't appealing at that moment. *I need to figure out where I am and go tell Joey about the passages.* She forced herself up off the ground and slowly opened the door. Peeking into a hallway she had never seen before; she drew in a sharp breath.

A spiral staircase at the end of the hall led up to one of the turrets. *I'm on the third floor.* She eyed the staircase, which consisted of thin wooden slats supported by an even thinner metal skeleton. The wooden slats didn't look very reliable, but the turret was calling to her.

Holding on tightly to the rickety staircase's thin handrail and carefully taking one step at a time, she watched in horror as it began to collapse behind her when she reached the landing. The sound, after the vacuum of the secret passage, seemed to boom like an explosion. The turret shook as dust and stinkers filled the air. *I'm stuck, but at least I wasn't on the stairs when they fell.*

She stared at the destruction for a moment, letting her breathing return to normal, then turned to inspect what had become her prison cell. The wall which housed the landing for the stairs was flat with three round sides boasting two large windows, a set of French doors, and a wrap-around balcony. *It's bigger than I expected.* A telescope sat in front of one of the windows, and Marge stooped to peer through the eye piece, surprised at the strength of the telescope and where it was pointed. *Someone has been watching who's coming and going.*

Her eyebrows rose. She turned and walked to the desk that sat against the flat wall. Sitting down on the office-style chair, she swung back and forth for a moment before looking in the drawers. But for an ancient looking book in the top drawer, the desk was empty.

She carefully opened the book and discovered it was a journal. The entries were made with a fountain pen, in ornate, cursive writing.

Mr. Abraham Rutherford's name was inscribed inside the front cover of the little book. Each entry was headed with a date, beginning with October 4, 1888. Fascinated, Marge began to read.

> *4.October.1888*
> *My darling Edith has accepted my proposal of marriage, so I am determined to build her a castle. M. Levesque has posted me architectural drawings. Building will commence next week. The builders are optimistic about laying the foundation before the first freeze.*

> *23.October.1888*
> *During the final stages of excavation for the basement, the builders have come upon a natural spring, which could result in difficulties. I have been asked to make a decision.*

Marge was finding Mr. Rutherford's handwriting somewhat tedious, and she wanted to find out about the curse, so she flipped ahead in the book, past the marriage and the completion of the mansion, past the birth of his children, until he met the caretaker's daughter.

> *17.June.1915*
> *I have met a dark-haired enchantress by the name of Anabelle. She was swimming in the hidden garden and did not take notice of my presence. A lovelier girl I have never seen and when she climbed out of the pond and blushed so prettily, I took leave of my senses and succumbed to her advances. Although I craved more of her company, she disappeared, and I never saw her again.*

4.July.1915

Anabelle's disappearance was precipitous. Edith and I have resumed our marital relations and she is with child. I do not believe she would have forgiven me for my indiscretion. I was lonely when we were having difficulties, but am much happier now, and I dare say she is happier as well.

30.August.1915

I met Jonathon by chance as I was strolling through the grounds. He accused me of impregnating his young daughter, and I denied it. He never mentioned her name. When he did, I was shocked. She is but fifteen and her name is Anabelle. What could I say in my own defense? Had I realized her age or her parentage, I would like to believe that I would have fought my baser instincts. But now, after she seduced me but once and my darling Edith pregnant, I was forced to deny his accusations. I do not think he believed me, but I told him he would have to find employment elsewhere and settled on him a generous sum.

Marge was incredulous. Fifteen? And he denied it? She paused and looked up. She imagined that she heard someone calling her name from a great distance. She listened closely but heard nothing but the wind howling outside the turret windows.

Chapter 12

Joey observed a slender woman with long, snowy-white hair walk, *float?* around the corner and cross the kitchen. She opened the refrigerator and took out the bag of sandwiches. Without thinking he said, "Those are mine."

Startled, the woman froze momentarily before dropping the bag. She ran. Joey got up stiffly and reached for his walker. He returned the bag to the refrigerator and looked in the direction the woman fled.

She had disappeared just like Freida described the night before. He texted Marge but received no answer. *I wonder if she dozed off.* He had been stationary for six hours and the cold kitchen was making his joints ache.

After several more attempts, he decided it was time to rouse her.

Making his way into the foyer, he ran into James descending the stairs. "Is Marge upstairs with Freida?"

"No, Freida's still sleeping so I left Paws with her."

"I wonder where she went." Joey peeked beneath the staircase and saw Marge's vacant chair.

"I'll start a new pot of coffee and help you look." James seemed unconcerned, but he didn't know Marge very well.

Joey was beginning to panic. "I'll start searching now. She's not answering my texts."

"Okay. I'll catch up with you. Maybe her battery died."

James headed for the kitchen as Joey limped to the ballroom, his stiff joints slowing him down. He looked in all the corners and through the French windows, suspecting that the alarm would have sounded had Marge opened any of the outside doors. He passed through the curtained alcove and into the sitting room, noticing the fire had gone out. The room was empty.

Searching the entire circumference of the ground floor, Joey rejoined James in the kitchen.

"Any luck?"

"No. No sign of her." He checked his phone again then headed back toward the door to the formal dining room.

James followed him through the dining room and into the study. Looking around carefully, he picked up Marge's phone from a bookcase shelf. "Is this her phone?"

"Yes. Where can she be?"

"Maybe she decided to look around upstairs."

Joey frowned. "That was not our plan. Why would she leave her phone here and not tell me where she was going?"

"Women." James shrugged. "I never know what they're thinking."

Joey was worried. He telephoned Peter and asked him to come.

The construction crew arrived with Hugh, and James turned off the alarm.

Freida came downstairs with Paws and began to make breakfast. "Where's Marge?"

Joey didn't want to alarm her, but James said, "She's disappeared. We can't find her."

Freida dropped the carton of eggs she was holding and stared at him. "We have to find her. Where have you looked? Get Hugh to help. Right. Now!"

A search party was formed and, although the alarm had been on, Joey went outside with the construction crew to look around the perimeter. With Marge, anything was possible.

<hr>

Completely absorbed and without her phone, Marge had no concept of time, but noticed the sun was almost directly overhead when she put the journal down. *I had better consider how I'm going to escape this room.*

She went through the French doors to the narrow balcony, which reminded her of a stone trough, with a waist-high wall around it. Bending over the wall, she peered down, unable to see any way to safely descend. It occurred to her that the balcony might crumble like the stairs, so she tested her footing and the strength of the wall as she circled.

Far below, she saw Joey walk around the corner of the house with someone in a hard hat. She tried yelling, but she was too far up, and the wind was drowning out any sound she made. She looked around for something she could drop but found nothing. *I don't want to destroy that book.* As a last-ditch effort, she removed her black polyester trousers and waved them like a flag.

The wall preserved her modesty, but a more vibrant color would surely have attracted attention more easily. It took a few minutes, and the wind tried to rip them from her grasp, but the moving fabric finally caught Joey's attention. She saw him look up, and could see his mouth move, but she couldn't hear what he said. He pointed and the other man, Hugh, she thought, looked up at her.

Marge pulled her pants back on and went back inside where she felt safer. She picked up the journal once again and continued to read while she waited to be rescued, for she had no doubt that Joey would come to her aid.

> *15.September.1915*
> *After the fire, I realized that the secret passages might not be adequate if my family needed to escape, so I contacted my original builders and asked them for assistance. I have also decided to hide a portion of our family wealth in a secure location. It will never be discovered, except by future generations who, if clever enough, might decipher the clues I leave in this journal.*

Hearing a commotion below, Marge set the book down and got up to look over the landing.

Hugh and his construction chief stood staring in horror at the destroyed staircase. He looked up, his eyes meeting those of Marge, and said, "How did you get up here? This floor was boarded up."

"There are secret passages running all through the house. Up and down, left and right, I am unsure if I could relocate this place."

"I've called for a fire truck, but I thought it might be quicker to come up here from inside. I didn't realize the stairs had collapsed. Are you safe up there?"

"Yes, I'm fine, except nature is calling."

"I think I hear the siren. Stay away from the landing, and we should be able to get you down shortly."

Hugh and the chief left, shaking their heads, and Marge scooted away from the ledge, relieved to hear that help was on the way. She went back out on the balcony and saw Joey below, looking up at her. She waved and smiled, to put him at ease, and watched the driver of the fire truck speak with him, and with Hugh, who had returned, before getting back in the truck and backing around the side of the house so he could extend the ladder.

Once the truck was in position, the ladder slowly extended to the top edge of the balcony wall. As she watched, a firefighter wearing a harness began the long climb toward her. When he got to the top, he helped her into a second harness and attached hers to his before descending first and guiding her to safety. Not particularly afraid of heights, Marge was nevertheless aware of the distance to the ground, and her legs felt wobbly beneath her, giving out when she reached the back of the truck and felt herself on solid ground.

When the firefighter turned to unhook their harnesses, Joey rushed toward Marge and attempted to help her from the truck. Holding onto his walker with one hand and bracing his legs, he reached out his other hand.

Unfortunately, one of Marge's unsteady feet missed the step and she fell, knocking Joey over in the process. The walker flipped to the side, instead of landing between them. Joey gasped, then groaned.

She quickly rolled off him and, on her knees, peered into his face. "Are you okay? What has transpired? You don't usually make those sounds when I land on you."

Joey was still for a moment, attempting to regulate his breathing, then said, "Your elbow."

"What about my elbow?"

"Nothing." He groaned again, then sat up.

Hugh approached and gave him a hand, retrieving his walker in the process, then turned to Marge. "Sergeant Locke is here now. Could you show us where you entered the secret passage?"

Joey's eyes widened. "Is that how you got up there?"

"Yes. There are many entrances and exits, but I found the entrance in the study. I'll bet that's how the 'ghost' got in and out of the kitchen." She got up off the ground. "Come on, I'll show you."

Leading the way into the house and through the study door, she walked to the end of the bookshelves and pulled out the three connected books. Peter entered the room with a deputy as the shelves swung outward. "You'll need flashlights," Marge said. "It's pitch-black inside."

"We have two objectives," Hugh said. "We need to find out where our intruder is entering the house, and we also need a map of the passages for inspection purposes. How do they work, Ms. Bumfuzzle?"

"The passage branches off to the left and right, with stairs leading up and down. I completely lost my bearings. There are exits, but each one has a catch, so when my flashlight broke, I got lost because I couldn't see how to open them."

"Your flashlight broke?" Peter's brow furrowed. "How did you get out?"

"I prayed." Marge shivered.

Hugh and the construction chief each paired with a police officer and, armed with flashlights, notepads, and pens, entered the passage in a single-file line. Marge and Joey watched them go, and Marge saw the entrance once again close of its own accord.

"Why didn't you text me before you went in there? I was very worried."

"I had no inkling it would wind all over the house. I'm starving. Do any sandwiches remain?"

"I think so. I stopped the ghost lady from pilfering them."

"You spoke to her? What did she say?"

"Nothing. She dropped the bag and ran. Let's go find out if they're still in the fridge because I'm hungry too."

"I found something," Marge said. She pulled out the journal she had found and handed it to Joey.

Flipping through it carefully, Joey whistled. "This must have been written by Abraham Rutherford, back in the late 1800s."

"Yes, and he wrote about the secret passages and hidden treasure. I am sure many people would like to acquire it."

"You've read it already?"

"Not all of it. I read a portion while I was incarcerated in the turret. That's a fascinating room, by the way."

"What's it like?"

Marge described the room, then stopped. "I forgot to tell you about the telescope. It was pointed at the front drive, so somebody could keep track of who's been coming and going. I guess I ruined access to their vantage point when the staircase went crashing down."

"You may have ruined their whole operation by finding the secret passages. They're no longer a secret." He chuckled. "How long do you think Hugh and Peter will be gone?"

"I have no idea. I completely lost track of time in there."

Chapter 13

When the secret passage exploration contingency returned with a hand-drawn map, they called a meeting in the kitchen. More coffee was passed around as James, who had returned from work, Freida, Joey, and Marge, all waited patiently to hear what they had to report.

Hugh held up his map and looked at it before speaking. "We followed all of the branches of the passage but didn't find an entrance to the house. We did find a locked door at the bottom, which could lead to a basement.

"As for the rest of the passage, it runs through each room and upstairs in several places, zigzagging around so it isn't noticeable. For someone who's had time to figure it out, it's probably easy to navigate. The only rooms we didn't find exits for were the kitchen, dining room, and ballroom."

"But there must be one in the kitchen, unless that lady really was a ghost," Freida exclaimed.

Glancing at her, Hugh continued, "Our first priority, for security, is to seal off the entrance to the house. We can't have an unknown person wandering through the passages. I asked one of the crew to place a padlock on the inside of the basement door so it can't be opened, and Sergeant Locke will be posting a deputy inside the kitchen tonight, so you should all be able to get a good night's sleep."

"That makes me feel a lot better. You're certain it's not a ghost?" Freida's brow furrowed.

"Very unlikely."

Before they split up, Marge approached Peter and told him about the book she found.

"Could you make two or three copies and see that it is locked up somewhere safe?" she asked. "It is of great historical value, and I'm afraid it might get stolen."

"Of course. What are the copies for?"

"The Rutherford who wrote it included information about the secret passages. It might be helpful."

Peter looked down at the small book he held and nodded. "I have to get back to the station, so I'll take care of it right away."

Freida crossed the room and joined them. "Sergeant Locke?" she asked timidly, "We've been planning a housewarming party for next weekend. Do you think we should cancel it?"

"I think it should be okay. The entrance to the passages has been blocked off and I doubt anything will happen with a lot of people here. How many are you inviting?"

"We have a long list. You're invited too, of course. We were planning to send out invitations today."

Marge silently listened to the exchange, hoping Peter was right.

"I apologize but I really need to get back to the station."

Freida thanked him and turned to Marge as he left. "You look worried. Do you think the party is a bad idea?"

"I am unsure. Perhaps the police will have the case resolved by then."

"Would you help me with the invitations? We've been so busy that I haven't had time."

"Truthfully, I'm exhausted. Do you think I could go home for a rest first?"

"Yes! Of course. I'm sorry. I forgot you were up all night. How about tomorrow morning?"

"What's happening tomorrow morning?" asked Joey, who had been studying Hugh's map.

"I will assist with party invitations."

"I'll drop you off after breakfast if you like. Are you ready to go home?"

Marge nodded wearily. "I'll see you tomorrow, Freida."

Joey dropped Marge off in front of her house, then parked the UTV in his driveway across the street. He went inside, turned up his thermostat and lit a fire before texting someone. "We're all clear for tomorrow morning. Be here at eleven. J."

He smiled and turned on the TV. *Marge will be so surprised. I can't wait for Christmas. We still have to get a tree.*

Although it was only six o'clock, the sky was dark, and he had been awake for nearly twenty-four hours. He dozed off in the middle of the historical documentary he was watching, starting awake three hours later. He sat very still. The doorknob rattled, then turned, and Seth walked in.

"Hi, Uncle Joey." He grinned, removing his coat, and hanging it in the hall closet. "I saw the light was on. Is it okay if I crash here tonight?"

Joey exhaled. "Of course. What time is it?"

"It's nine. My friends had to go home, and my dad's at work tonight, so I thought... do you have anything to eat?"

Chuckling, Joey rose from his recliner and grabbed his walker. "Come with me. I have leftover sandwiches from last night."

Trailing him into the kitchen, Seth sat at the kitchen table. "Why are you home so early? I thought you'd be at Aunt Marge's house, but all her lights are off."

"We were on a midnight stakeout at the Rutherford place last night. I'd be sleeping too but I fell asleep watching TV."

"I'm sorry I woke you up. You and Aunt Marge are like superheroes." Seth grinned and took a section of sandwich from the pile Joey placed on a plate.

"I'm glad you did. If I slept all night on that recliner, I'd be stiff as a board in the morning." Feeling mildly peckish himself, Joey helped himself to a sandwich.

Marge woke early the next morning and groaned. She made her way downstairs to feed Fluster and stopped to take two ibuprofen. She looked around her kitchen and sighed. After all the work she put into her imaginary island paradise, it had gotten very little use and was inconvenient. She started a pot of coffee and began clearing up her decorations. She had already emptied the wading pool after Fluster accidentally deflated it with a claw, so with a little shifting of plants and decorations, she was able to return the dining table to its proper location and reclaim her kitchen counter. *Christmas will be here before we know it. We'll have to get a tree.*

When she logged onto Facetime for yoga, Joey wasn't waiting for her. She checked her clock and furrowed her brow. *He must be very tired.* She sent him a text and waited. No answer. She sent him a second text, "I'll start breakfast. Come over when you're up."

She took a quick shower, examined her bruised posterior, dressed in her new, cerise pantsuit, and hobbled back downstairs.

Pouring herself a cup of coffee, she placed a record from her Big Band Era collection on the record player and began extracting pancake ingredients from her pantry.

⁘⁘⁘

Joey entered to the sound of Marge's slightly off-key rendition of 'Flat Foot Floogie.' He rounded the corner to the kitchen, and although he was virtually nose blind, he knew what was for breakfast. The pancake bowl was out, and he heard the sound of sizzling bacon. "Mm pancakes and bacon."

Turning abruptly from the stove, Marge said, "How did you know?"

"Visual cues." Joey grinned lopsidedly. "I'm sorry I missed yoga."

"You haven't had much sleep lately. How are you feeling this morning?"

"Much better."

He sat at the table and accepted the large plate of pancakes and bacon Marge set in front of him. Adding a cup of coffee, she said, "Would you like eggs, too?"

"This is plenty. Thank you. Have you eaten already?"

"No. I'll just add some batter and join you."

"What time did Freida ask you to come?"

"She didn't specify." Removing her apron, Marge joined Joey at the table.

Once he had filled his gastronomic void, he eyed Marge's dazzling pantsuit. "Is that a new outfit?"

"Yes. I bought it for Christmas. What do you think?"

"It's very festive." His eyes twinkled.

Marge grinned. "Would you like another cup of coffee?"

"Yes, please." He waited until she returned his cup. "We need to get a tree."

"I was pondering that as well. Maybe tomorrow? We could visit the tree farm." The outing was something of a ritual. The hayride, looking through the gift shop, hot cider, and a freshly made apple pie to bring home added to the fun.

"That will get us into the spirit. We can listen to Christmas music on the way."

"Let's get a giant tree this year."

"Marge…"

"Pleeeease?"

"That will require you to climb a ladder. How will we even get it up?"

"Perhaps Peter will assist. Or Seth. Please?"

"We'll see." Joey smiled at her enthusiasm. This conversation, too, was an annual ritual.

⸎

Marge arrived at Rutherford Mansion at ten thirty and rang the bell. Freida answered and took her coat before ushering her into the kitchen.

"Where's Paws?" Marge asked, over the sound of thumping, loud voices, and country music emanating from upstairs.

"I gave him a bone, so he's occupied. Sorry about the noise. How are you feeling this morning?"

"Much improved. How about you? Did you have a restful night?"

"Yes. Having the deputy here helped a lot."

"No midnight intruders, then?"

"No. Everything was quiet, speaking of which…" Freida shut the kitchen door, cutting the noise considerably. "Would you like a cup of coffee before we begin?"

Marge considered her coffee consumption for a moment. "Yes, an additional cup would be welcome. How extensive is your guestlist?"

Freida carried two cups of coffee to the table and picked up a list. "I have two hundred people on the list, but some of them are couples, and I've addressed about three dozen. I'm crossing them out as I go."

"You can eliminate Joey and me; we will be here and don't need an invitation."

"We'll send you one anyway, as a memento. Here's the box of invitations and pens. We can each take a page and get started if you like." She placed her hand on Marge's. "I really appreciate all your help. I don't know what I would do without you."

"I'm happy to assist."

"Millicent and Harriet are going to help with decorating tomorrow, if you'd like to come."

"I would, but Joey and I are going to Lee's tomorrow to get a tree."

"How fun! We're going to get ours this evening. I'm sure we'll still be decorating day after tomorrow so come whenever you have time."

Marge nodded, picking up a pen and extracting several invitations.

Chapter 14

The next morning, bundled in long underwear, heavy coats, hats, gloves, and scarves, Marge and Joey set off in the UTV for Lee's Christmas tree farm. Marge was in high spirits, and they enjoyed the ride, singing loudly to the Christmas CD she had brought along. Joey had decked out the UTV in Christmas garlands and battery-operated lights so passengers in the cars that passed them good-naturedly honked and waved.

The tree farm parking lot was sparsely populated on the weekday morning, so Joey parked near the entrance. He found this particular ritual somewhat taxing, but enjoyed it immensely, nevertheless.

Passing through the gift shop, they bought tickets for the hayride and picked out wreaths that would be ready when they returned, then they tromped up the hill out back, to catch their ride. His walker lacked traction on the uphill gravel, so Marge held onto the left handle to make sure it didn't slide backwards.

"Look, they're waiting for us." She pointed at the tractor hitched to a trailer full of hay.

As they approached, the driver greeted them and placed a small set of steps with a handrail next to an opening in the trailer's safety rail. Marge took Joey's walker as he climbed the steps and situated himself in the hay, then handed it up so she could climb.

"Do you know what kind of tree you're looking for? Since it's just the two of you, we don't need to stop in every lot, and I can wait while you choose your tree."

Joey looked at Marge. "Douglas, I think."

She nodded.

"Okay. Get comfortable. Next stop, the Douglas forest." He placed the steps in the back of the trailer and climbed aboard the tractor.

A speaker began to play 'Jingle Bells,' and Marge and Joey alternately sang and laughed as they bounced up and down on the hay.

"This is much more fun when we're the only passengers." Marge bounced high and winced as the trailer hit a pothole in the dirt road.

"More comfortable too, not having to worry about landing on someone else's boot." Joey paused. "What's wrong, Marge?"

"Nothing. I'm fine." Her eyes teared.

"I can see that you're not."

"I slipped in the secret passage and fell. I'm much improved, but that last bounce was painful. I think the ibuprofen might be wearing off."

"I didn't even ask about your adventure. I was only thinking about how worried I'd been. What can I do to help?"

"You don't happen to have your hip flask, do you?"

Joey pulled the flask out of his coat pocket and handed it to her. "Maybe you could lay back in the hay or roll onto your side. Would that help?"

"It might." Marge took a few sips from the flask then rolled onto her side, her face gradually relaxing. "Thanks, Joey."

The trailer came to a stop amidst a grid of Douglas firs, ranging from tiny seedlings to towering giants. The driver helped them disembark and sat to wait.

Marge glanced around and headed for an eleven-foot-tall tree, Joey trailing her with foreboding.

"Marge…"

"Just kidding." She grinned. "Do you see one you like?"

He looked around, then pointed to a beautiful little tree. "What about that one?"

"It's very small."

"They look smaller than they are out here. Besides, the shape is nice."

Marge looked like she was about to pout, but then her eyes lit up, and she hobbled toward another tree.

"Look! This is our tree. It's just a little bit bigger than that one, and it's perfect." She walked all the way around it, tipping her head back to see the top.

Joey leaned on his walker and eyed the tree. It was beautiful. Six or seven feet tall. Following Marge around the tree he nodded. "I think you're right. This is definitely our tree."

Marge hugged him and waved at their driver, who approached with a chainsaw. "Found your tree?"

Nodding happily, Marge watched as he lowered his safety glasses, pulled the cord on his chainsaw, and approached the tree. The noise was deafening, and she had to lean into Joey's walker to hear him.

"Let's go back to the trailer and get you comfortable for the return trip," he shouted.

She trailed behind him to the steps and stiffly climbed into the hay before taking his walker and rolling onto her side. Once he had joined her and the driver had placed the tree on the opposite side of the trailer, the music resumed, and they headed back to the entrance.

When the tractor came to a halt on the hill above the gift shop, the driver once again helped them disembark and handed Joey a ticket. "I'll get your tree ready to go."

"Thank you very much." Joey handed the driver a five-dollar bill and wished him a Merry Christmas, then allowed Marge to help him navigate the gravel hill. Descending was not much easier than ascending, the gravel wreaking havoc.

He knew that Marge would be busy looking at ornaments and other hand-crafted items for quite some time, so he bought a cup of hot apple cider and a donut and found a bench.

He jolted awake when Marge sat next to him with a cup of cider and offered him another donut. "I must have dozed off. Did you find everything you wanted?"

She nodded, her mouth full. "Except for our special ornament. You must help me choose."

"I almost forgot about that."

Every year they picked one special ornament to add to their tree, something that reminded them of their year together.

Finishing their donuts and cider, they put the cups and wrappers in the trash receptacle and wandered toward the rows of ornaments. They searched and discussed various ornaments before Joey stopped and plucked one that was misplaced. It was a man and woman in formal wear, dancing a waltz. "This one."

Marge stood next to him and studied it. The dark-haired man wore a tuxedo, and the woman had a bun and wore an evening gown with glitter. "Beautiful."

"It reminds me of dancing under the fairy lights on your back patio."

"And at the festival last summer."

"And we'll be dressed up for the housewarming party this weekend."

"Let's get it. It's perfect. Now all we lack are the pie and the wreaths, then we can check out."

"You pick out the pie. I'll get the wreaths and lay them on my basket. Here. Don't forget the tree." He handed her the ticket. "I'll meet you at the register.

Once they had paid for their items and loaded them in the UTV, Joey drove up the hill and parked at the tree-loading zone. Marge hopped out and handed their ticket to the boy who was helping prep the trees, and Joey walked to the back with a couple of bungee cords.

Once the tree was secure, they headed back down the hill. "Joey, I am desirous of additional cider and donuts."

"I think what you really want is some lunch."

Marge paused and thought about that. "You're probably right, but we've got to get the tree home now." She paused again. "I'll make grilled cheese and tomato soup. I have eggnog, too. I will text Peter and ask if he is able to assist with the installation of the tree."

<hr>

"Just say when," Peter texted back.

He was parked in her driveway when they got home.

"You are speedy."

"I'm hungry." He laughed.

"Yours is first on the grill." She let herself into the house and completely forgot about Fluster's new greeting.

Reeling backward when he launched himself from the back of the sofa, she began a chain reaction. She slammed against Peter's back, which propelled the tree in Joey's direction and knocked him backward off the bottom step.

Turning to see if Peter was alright, she joined him gaping at Joey, who had fortuitously landed in the grass.

"You'll be the death of me, Marge." He chuckled. "But what a fun way to go."

"I'm so sorry." She rushed to help him up. "I neglected to consider Fluster's assault. Are you injured?" She tugged on his hand a little too hard and would have fallen backward if Peter hadn't caught her.

Shaking his head, Peter said, "You two are going to hurt each other if you're not more careful."

They managed to get the tree in the house, and Marge quickly prepared lunch while Peter positioned it in the stand. Sitting around the table, Marge asked, "Are you planning to spend Christmas with us this year?"

"I would, Aunt Marge, but I requested time off to visit my grandparents. I haven't seen them for a long time."

"I'm sure they'll love having you visit, but we'll miss you."

"We can have a mini-Christmas when I get back."

Laying her hand on his, Marge smiled. "I'd like that."

Joey laid his spoon down. "Has anything happened at the Rutherford place since Marge found the secret passage?"

"Not a thing. The deputies I've posted on night duty have started grumbling about it being a waste of time, so I'm thinking about pulling them for the time being. Maybe I'll wait until after the party, just to be sure."

On the day before the party, Marge sat at Freida's kitchen table with her friends. Millicent had brought expertly baked scones, homemade jam, and clotted cream for a treat, and Harriet brewed a special pot of English breakfast tea.

"These are so delicious, Millicent. I still want you to give me baking lessons when the weather improves." Harriet took a big bite of her scone.

"I'm glad you like them. It's been a long time since I had anyone to bake for." She turned to Freida. "The dessert and wine idea is brilliant."

"That was Marge's idea."

"The party will be a little late for dinner." Marge nodded, chewing enthusiastically.

"Millicent volunteered to bring canapes and servers." Freida smiled. "That will give the party some class. Thank you all for helping me decorate."

"We were glad to assist." Marge sipped her tea.

"What is everyone wearing tomorrow night?" Freida asked suddenly.

"I have a closet full of ballgowns from years gone by," Millicent said. "I'm just going to close my eyes and pick one."

Chapter 15

The following evening, Marge sighed dreamily as Joey pulled up in front of Rutherford mansion and parked the UTV. "It looks exactly like a fairytale castle."

"And you look like the princess." Joey winked at her.

Lights, music, and happy chatter greeted them before they strode through the grand, front entrance, but once inside, Marge's senses reeled. She stood motionless amidst the whorl of sound, color, motion, and scents. Two hundred voices echoed inside the stone walls. Colorful, sequined gowns moved through the foyer, reflecting thousands of fairy lights. Wood fires, pine, food, and perfume vied for attention. Marge stinkered.

Joey took one hand off his walker and placed it on her elbow, helping her back outside. He stood close to her and turned her to face him. "Marge."

Marge blinked.

"Are you okay?"

"Of course. I'm fine."

Joey remained silent.

"That was somewhat overwhelming."

"We can go home if you want to."

Breathing in deeply through her nose and pressing her lips together, Marge shook her head. "I want to be here."

"How can I help?"

"Maybe I will be okay now. It was just so unexpected. We could commence from this location, listening and watching from a distance."

"I could bring you a drink and a small plate of food."

Marge nodded and was surprised when Joey returned with more than food.

Harriet and Pastor Greg accompanied him. "I thought we might also introduce a couple of friends into the equation." He handed her a drink and a plate.

Taking a sip of her drink, Marge gave a wobbly smile and blinked rapidly.

"You look beautiful, Marge. Who'd have thought you'd clean up so nice?" Harriet winked at her.

"Thank you, Harriet. You look lovely too." Marge looked questioningly at Joey, wondering if he had told them what happened.

"There's quite a lot of commotion in there, but it's pretty cold out here, so we'll see you inside. I just wanted to say hello." Harriet smiled and gave Marge a little hug before she and Greg rejoined the party.

"I didn't say anything," Joey reassured her. "I just told them we were waiting for the foyer to clear out a little."

Marge took another sip of her drink and looked at him over the rim of her glass. "I'm grateful you're here with me," she said. "You rescued me."

"You rescued me in the yogurt tank. That's what friends do."

Rapidly blinking again, Marge smiled. "So. Here we are outside, witnessing a marvelous party. We can hear the music and voices from here."

"I see lots of lights. I think you helped hang them."

"I did." Marge nodded.

"Let's move a little closer."

As they gradually moved closer to the entrance, guests began filtering into the other downstairs rooms, leaving the foyer less chaotic.

Entering the house a second time, Marge felt much more relaxed.

Freida approached with a happy smile and gave Marge a hug. "You made it work! Your dress is wonderful."

Hugging her back then twirling around, Marge's eyes twinkled.

Her long, sparkling gown of sea foam blue swirled around her, and her curly hair flowed down her back. For once, her eyelashes were where they belonged, and she had carefully applied her makeup.

"Help yourselves to the hors d'oeuvres," Freida said. "The desserts are on the buffet table over there." She indicated the table and turned to greet Hugh.

Marge was about to suggest they dance, when the front doors opened, and Mark Stubbs entered with Sayuri on his arm. She glanced at Joey to see if he saw them, but he merely shrugged.

"Ready to hit the dance floor? I think I might hear KC and the Sunshine Band."

They got as far as the ballroom doors when Marge looked back and saw Freida's mother in the front entrance. "Ooh. She looks so beautiful."

"Who?" Joey stopped and turned. "Did Freida know she was coming?"

"I don't know, but she's here with Chief Lloyd and heading in Mark's direction. I hope there won't be any trouble."

Peter approached. "Good evening, Aunt Marge, Joey." He turned to see what they were looking at.

"A curious couple. How did they meet?"

"My fault, actually. Freida said her mother needed a date and the chief hasn't been out much since his wife died, so I introduced them. Was that a bad idea?"

"I don't know." Marge tilted her head slightly, watching Chief Lloyd and Mark shake hands and their dates give each other stiff smiles. "It could go either way. She seems to be on her best behavior tonight."

"Fingers crossed. You two have fun." Peter left them and after another moment, Joey said, "Come on Marge. Let's get in there before the song's over."

·· ⊂⊂⊃⊃ ··

Joey loved seeing Marge enjoy herself and was chuckling at her antics when a long, shimmering sheath of silver sequins caught his eye. A newcomer, balding and rotund in a custom fit tuxedo, crossed the ballroom floor with the tall, lithe woman in the sparkling gown, stopping to address Millicent, who was sedately dancing near Marge and him.

"Hello, Douglas, I'm glad you could make it."

"Thank you for inviting me." He took her hand. "Nicky, this is Millicent Beaumonde. Millicent, this is my friend Nicky."

"It's nice to meet you, Mrs. Beaumonde."

Marge noticed that Mr. Taft's friend wasn't given a surname and wondered why, but having made introductions, he took her arm and continued across the room in Mark and Sayuri's direction. They were staring at him as he approached their location near the curtained alcove. Douglas said something that made Mark take a step back and stiffen. His reply caused Douglas' beady eyes to narrow and his florid face to flush a dark, ugly color.

Joey began easing Marge toward the door as Douglas stepped closer and Mark's hand balled into a fist. He wondered if he should intervene when he saw James stride purposely into the ballroom and pause to scan the guests. He caught sight of Mark and Douglas and rushed past Joey when the lights went out.

A brief moment of complete silence ensued. Standing very still, Joey listened. Then the rustling and voices began as partygoers reacted to the sudden darkness. He heard Marge's string of nervous flatulence. He called her name and put his hand out to take hers, but someone ran by him, giving him a shove. He tried to use his walker to stop his momentum, but he lost his grip as he flew sideways, and he heard Marge's cry as his shoulder connected and the thunk as her head hit the floor. Breathing heavily, he lay on top of her and didn't know what to do. He couldn't see anything in the darkness. "Marge?" he whispered. "Marge, are you okay?"

"I am not yet certain. Could you possibly relocate? I am unable to draw breath."

Feeling around for solid ground, he pushed himself up and scooted off her. "Just stay there until the lights come back on."

Marge groaned.

--------·-·⟨∞⟩-·--------

The lights were blinding when they went on. Marge remained on the floor and blinked at Joey as he pushed himself to his knees and studied her with a worried frown. A woman began to scream.

"Someone call an ambulance," James shouted.

Millicent and Harriet approached and looked down at Marge. "Are you okay? What happened?"

"The ambulance isn't for me, is it? Can someone help me up?" Marge lifted her arms, and her friends helped her to her feet.

Joey struggled to his feet as well. "Are you hurt, Marge? I'm so sorry about that."

Marge straightened her dress and glanced around, trying to figure out what was going on. "I'll live, but what's happening? There's Peter." She limped a little as she strode across the ballroom, the others following her.

Sayuri was on her knees next to Mark, who lay on his back with a knife protruding from his abdomen. James held Freida in his arms, attempting to console her as Peter spoke urgently into his radio.

Without a thought, Marge dropped to her knees and put her arms around Sayuri. She stiffened momentarily, then laid her head against Marge's shoulder as she sobbed. Looking up at Peter, Marge raised her brows in question.

"He's still alive. The ambulance will be here in a minute."

"Can Sayuri ride with him to the hospital?"

"We'll ask when they get here."

--------·-·⟨∞⟩-·--------

Standing at the edge of the circle gathered around the tableau, Joey felt a lump in his throat as he watched Marge.

He moved aside as the crowd shifted to let the paramedics through. Marge remained by Sayuri's side until she climbed into the ambulance and stood watching as the lights disappeared into the darkness.

Approaching her quietly, Joey stood next to her, leaning on his walker. When she turned her head, he was surprised by the haunted look in her eyes. "Are you alright?"

"Yes. I hope he survives," she said, her voice barely a whisper.

Chapter 16

The crime scene technicians arrived at the mansion just behind the ambulance. Peter had photographed the scene before the paramedics loaded Mark onto the gurney. He approached James and Freida. "Do you have a guest list available?"

"Yes. I'll get it for you." Freida left the room.

"Bloom, when Mrs. Nelson returns, you and Carter take the guest list to the front entrance," he addressed his deputies. "Before anyone leaves, find them on the list and inquire if they were in the ballroom when the lights went out. If they were, ask them where they were standing and take notes. If they were anywhere near the victim, ask them to wait to be interviewed."

Freida reappeared with a sheaf of papers and handed them to Peter, who passed them to deputy Bloom. He then scanned the small crowd and asked James and Freida to join him in the curtained alcove. He sat on an upholstered chair and indicated the loveseat.

James wore his stoic expression, and Freida looked frightened and grief stricken. "Will he make it?" she asked.

"I can't make any promises, but he was stable when he was taken to the hospital."

"Thank goodness!"

James took her shaky hand in his.

"Could you give me your version of what happened?"

"Freida came and got me in the foyer because her father and another man were arguing, and she was worried they might get into a fight. I was just heading over to talk to them when the lights went out."

Peter stopped writing in his notebook and looked up. "What happened when the lights went out?"

"People were whispering and moving around but it was all very disorienting without light."

"How close were you to the victim?"

"I don't know. Maybe five or six yards?"

"Were you with James?"

"No. I followed, but he was moving much quicker than I was. He made it about halfway across the room when everything went dark." Tears were trickling down her cheeks.

"Who do you think might have done this?"

James and Freida looked at each other then back at Peter. "We didn't know the man he was arguing with," James said, "but when the lights came back on, he was gone."

"Did you discover why the lights went out?"

"No. It was strange. I don't even know where the breaker box is."

"I'll ask Mr. Rutherford about that. Did you know his date?"

"Who's? Mark's?"

"Yes. Sayuri."

"We met her once before."

Peter nodded. "That's all for now. I'm sorry we'll be here for a while, but you can move about the house now if you like."

"Thank you, Sergeant. Can I get you anything?" Freida asked.

"No, thank you, but could you send Marge and Joey in next?"

After they left, Peter sighed. It was going to be a long night.

<hr>

Eying Peter with trepidation, Marge held the curtain aside for Joey to pass through. They sat across from him and waited.

"Could you tell me your recollection of events?"

Joey glanced at Marge. "We were dancing near Millicent when a man named Douglas arrived with his date. He stopped to say hello to Millicent, and we were introduced. Then he walked over to Mark and Sayuri."

Marge nodded and touched her head, somewhat surprised by the tender bump she found there.

"How far away were you standing from Mr. Stubbs?"

"He was standing near here, in front of the curtain, and we were closer to the center of the room."

"It's a large room." Peter frowned.

"If you divide the room into quadrants, Petey, we were in Mark's quadrant."

"So, you could see his interaction with Douglas. Could you hear them?"

"No. The music was deafening."

"What's wrong with your head?"

"Nothing." Marge withdrew her hand from the lump.

"We had a little accident when the lights went out," Joey said.

"Do you need to see a doctor?"

"No, I'm fine."

Peter studied her for a moment then glanced at his notebook. "Douglas, Mark, and their dates were standing near the alcove. Did the two of you know their dates?"

"Sayuri is my ex-wife. Neither of us had met Douglas' date, Nicky, I think he said."

"Your ex-wife? That's quite a coincidence, isn't it? Did you know she would be here?"

"I didn't, but I might have guessed. Mark brought her here last week when he came to see Freida."

"Did you feel jealous?"

Marge, sitting next to him, felt him flinch slightly. "I haven't seen her for years."

"You didn't answer the question."

"I was not jealous, but I do wonder why she's here."

Marge leaned forward. "Mark said she's married to his business partner."

"Hmm." Peter tapped his pen against his lip. "Tell me about their interaction before the blackout."

"The men were standing very close and looked angry," Marge offered.

"What gave you that impression?"

She tilted her head, and her hand reached for the lump before she could stop herself.

Peter pressed his lips together.

"I couldn't see details from our location, but something about their body language looked unfriendly."

"What happened when the lights went out? Tell me about your accident."

"I suggested we should go get some refreshments, and we were moving toward the door." Joey looked at Marge.

"I was shocked and afraid to move," Marge took over the narrative. "Time seemed to stand still for a second, then everyone moved and spoke at the same time. I heard Joey call my name, then we were flying through the air."

"Someone ran into me. They were moving fast and hit me from the side. I tried to grab my walker, but I fell and landed on Marge." Joey turned. "I heard your head hit the floor, and I was so worried, but I couldn't see anything."

Marge grinned. "I've landed on you so many times I've lost count. It was your turn for a soft landing."

Peter rolled his eyes. "Describe the scene when the lights came back on."

"Someone screamed, I think. Marge was lying on the ground. My walker was on its side behind me. I was facing away from the alcove."

"All I saw was the ceiling and Joey, then Millicent and Harriet came over and offered assistance. When I regained an upright position, I heard someone shout for an ambulance and saw a crowd form near the alcove."

Peter looked up as Chief Lloyd entered.

"I was wondering where you were."

The chief perched on the edge of an easy chair. "I find myself in an uncomfortable position."

Peter glanced at Marge, who was nodding. "You're here with the victim's ex-wife."

"Well, his daughter's mother in any case, and she wasn't with me when he was stabbed." He hunched his shoulders and frowned.

"I think you can put your mind at ease," Joey said. "I didn't see her anywhere near the victim before the lights went out."

"But where was she? She might have been just behind us or over to the side where we weren't looking."

"The lights were only out for a minute and people were moving around. It would have been difficult to move across the room, find your target, and get away again in the dark. We could try to reenact it with a blindfold."

Chief Lloyd sighed. "Locke, you're in charge of this one. Even though I don't know Caroline very well, she is my date, and it could be considered a conflict of interest."

"Yes, sir. I can interview her next if you'd like to take her home."

"Thank you." Turning to Marge he said, "You stay out of this investigation."

"Of course." She smiled sweetly.

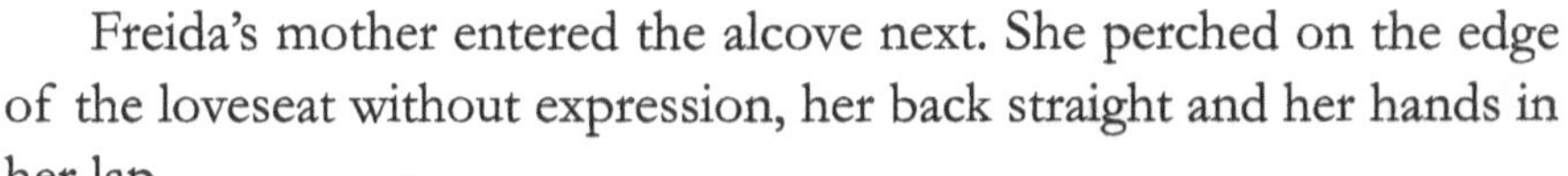

Freida's mother entered the alcove next. She perched on the edge of the loveseat without expression, her back straight and her hands in her lap.

"Could you tell me your full name and relation to Mark Stubbs please?"

"Caroline Gottlieb. He is my daughter's father."

"Do the two of you have an amicable relationship?"

"No, we do not. We haven't spoken for years."

Peter looked up from his notebook.

"We spoke briefly when I came to visit Freida, and he was here."

"Did you argue?"

"I don't know why you have to rehash things you already know."

"I want to hear your version."

Peter didn't know anything but listened intently.

"We didn't really argue. I just asked why he was here. I was angry with Freida for inviting him."

"You dislike him?"

"If you must know, he was having an affair when I was pregnant with Freida and was with his girlfriend when I was in the hospital giving birth. I called off our engagement and moved in with my parents until I could support myself and take care of her. It was a long time ago, but I'll never forgive him."

"Were you jealous of his date?"

"I certainly don't want him. Good luck to her is all I can say."

"Where were you when the lights went out?"

"I was sitting in the study waiting for my date to return with a drink. Your superior, I believe?"

"Yes, ma'am. And did he return?"

"After the lights came back on, I went to look for him and found him in line at the bar."

"Thank you. Is there anything you'd like to add?"

Looking away, she asked, "Will he be okay?"

"I believe so."

She nodded and stood. "Are we finished here?"

"Yes. Thank you very much."

Peter finished interviewing the guests who had been closest to the crime scene, then drove to the hospital to speak with Sayuri. After consulting with the doctor on call, he found her in the waiting room, staring at nothing.

Looking up as he entered, her shoulders slumped when she saw it was him. "Have you heard anything about Mark's condition?"

"Yes, the surgery was successful, and the doctor believes he'll make a full recovery."

Smiling with relief, Sayuri placed her hand on her heart.

"Is now a good time for our interview?"

"Yes. It's fine."

"Could I have your full name please?"

"Sayuri O'Donnell."

"You were Mr. Stubbs' date this evening?"

"Yes."

"Could you tell me how you know him?"

"He's my husband's business partner."

"Did you see who stabbed him?"

She shook her head. "The lights went out."

"Do you remember who was near you when they went out?"

"That fat man and his girlfriend were there. No one else was very close. I didn't really know anyone at the party."

"I understand Joey Cattywampus is your ex-husband. And you met several of the guests previously." Peter studied her face.

"I did know Joey, a lifetime ago. As for the others, I don't really know them even though we've met."

"Who do you think might want Mark dead?"

"No one! Why would they?"

"He didn't have any enemies?"

"Not that I know of."

"What were he and Mr. Taft arguing about?"

"I don't know. Some real estate deal."

"Where did Mr. Taft and his date go after Mr. Stubbs was injured?"

"I don't know. They were gone when the lights went on."

"Where are you staying?"

"At Mark's house. I don't know what to do now."

"Did he give you a key?"

She nodded.

"Just go ahead and stay there for now. Hopefully he'll be home soon."

"Thank you," she said quietly. "Is that all?"

"For now. Please don't leave town." Peter stood and left her to her thoughts.

<hr>

Marge, flushed and slightly tipsy, sat on the sofa in the sitting room next to Joey with her feet up. He leaned over and plucked an errant eyelash off her forehead and handed it to her.

Sitting across from them, Freida leaned her head against James' shoulder and sighed. "It was a lovely party, don't you think? Until dad got stabbed." She frowned prettily.

"Absolutely wonderful." Marge glanced at Joey, who nodded.

"Have you heard anything about his condition?"

"The doctor said he made it through surgery and that someone would call when we can visit." James squeezed Freida's hand.

"I'm just finally getting to know him." She closed her eyes and took a deep breath. "He's going to be fine. I have to believe that."

"Not as many people die of stab wounds as they make out in the movies. Death is usually caused by multiple stab wounds or twisting or pulling out the knife," Joey said.

Freida's eyes widened, and Marge elbowed him. "Those things didn't happen though, did they? I'm sure he will make a full recovery."

"Anyone for another?" James held up his glass.

"I think I've probably had enough," Marge said.

"Me too. I still have to navigate the woods."

"You can stay over if you like."

"I think I would like to go home and change if Joey's able to drive.

I wanted to wear this dress for Christmas, and it has already had a hard night."

A tap on the door preceded Harriet and Millicent's entrance. "We just wanted to thank you for a lovely party and let you know we'll be praying for your father," Harriet said. "We've spoken with the police, and I'm giving Millicent a ride home."

"Thank you. Both of you." Freida rose and gave them each a hug, tears threatening again.

"Let's have another party for Christmas, a makeup party, when your father has recovered."

"That's a marvelous suggestion, Millicent." Marge's grin was contagious, and everyone's spirits were lifted. "Joey and I should probably head home as well. Let's all have lunch on Sunday."

They all agreed without having to ask where.

Chapter 17

Saturday was meant to be a quiet day. Marge and Joey had been up late, and both agreed that a sleep in was required. Unfortunately, Peter didn't get the memo and, having been up all night himself, it didn't occur to him that they might be sleeping.

Pounding on Marge's front door at eight o'clock, he impatiently tapped his foot, then rang the doorbell. *Where is she? She can't have gone out already.* He rang the bell again, pulling out his phone and texting her. "Where are you Aunt Marge?" A few minutes later, he got her reply.

"Sleeping. Go away."

"Please get up. It's important."

Five frowning emojis, but he heard her thumping down the stairs. The lock turned and there stood Marge in her pajamas, wild red hair and streaked eye liner from the night before. Her accusatory look dented his resolve, but he needed her input.

"I'm sorry, Aunt Marge. I know you were up late."

"Come in, Petey. Have you slept at all?"

"No, not yet. Where's Joey?"

Marge rubbed her eyes, further distributing the eye liner. "I imagine he's in his own bed, sleeping uninterrupted." She frowned. "Do you need some coffee?"

"Yes, please. I might not get to sleep for a while. Here are two copies of that book, by the way. I thought you might want one for Joey too."

"Thank you." She started a pot of coffee and texted Joey: Petey's here if you're up.

She sat down across from Peter and waited. "Well?"

Placing his head in his hands, Peter groaned.

97

Marge poured him some coffee and went to answer Joey's knock. Pouring two more cups, she brought the coffee, milk, and sugar to the table before getting reseated.

"What's going on, Peter?"

"There are so many variables in this case, I hardly know where to start."

"You need to have a little faith in yourself." Joey sipped his coffee. "Who are your suspects?"

"Sayuri, Douglas, and Nicky seem to be the only people who were close enough, but there were other people there who might have wanted to see him dead."

"Such as?"

"Freida's mother. James? Who knows?"

Marge, who had been busy doctoring her coffee, said, "They were standing very near the alcove."

"What is that supposed to mean?"

"Only a curtain separates the alcove from the ballroom. Do you know who was in that room?"

Peter gaped at her and closed his eyes momentarily. "It just keeps getting better."

"Have you discovered any information about Douglas?"

"Douglas Taft, acquaintance of Millicent, property developer and gallery owner from Chesterville."

"Have you found him or his date?"

"No, and his car is still parked at the mansion."

"Where could someone go and not leave the house?"

"I know Aunt Marge, but how would he even know about the passages? And how would he leave the room… with his date?"

"There's that alcove." Marge paused. "Or there's that person who shoved Joey out of the way."

Peter stared at her.

"Just a thought." She shrugged.

On an entirely different wavelength, Joey asked, "Have you found out anything about the weapon?"

"It was about six inches long and came from the kitchen. No prints."

"And the wound?"

"He was stabbed by someone tall and strong."

"That should narrow it down a little. Will he recover?" Marge asked.

"Yes, the surgery went well. What should I do now?"

"Find Mr. Taft and get some sleep. Our brains don't function properly when we don't sleep."

"Said after you ply me with three cups of coffee."

"I did ask first."

Peter smiled. "Thanks, you guys. I appreciate your help. I'd better go now."

After he left, Marge and Joey remained at the table, sipping their coffee. "I didn't wake you, did I?"

"No, I was already awake."

"I thought you might be."

"What now? Are you going back to bed?"

"I imagine it's pointless. Perhaps I can take a nap later. Shall I make breakfast?"

"Why don't you go get dressed and I'll make breakfast?"

"Thank you." Marge grinned. "Wait about fifteen minutes before you start so I can take a shower."

"Will do. I'll feed Fluster too."

Marge trudged upstairs, feeling groggier by the minute. She really wanted a bath, but knew she'd probably fall asleep in the tub, so she took a quick shower, turning the water temperature to cold before she got out. That woke her up.

Shivering as she dressed in her lavender pant suit, she wrapped her hair in a towel and put on thick socks and warm slippers before returning downstairs. Smelling bacon as she rounded the corner, her stomach rumbled.

"The bacon smells divine." She grabbed a piece on the way to the coffee pot.

"I'm glad you think so because I made a lot of it."

"You can't smell it at all?"

"It's one of those things that I can almost smell." He set two plates on the table. "I don't know if it's because the smell is strong, or if it's just a memory."

"Maybe we should experiment. Did the doctors ever say if it's permanent?"

"No. They said there were too few cases to get any verifiable data. Eating would be a lot more fun if I could smell things." He picked up a piece of bacon and took a bite. "What are we going to do today?"

"I don't know. I did not intend to be up this early."

"We could have a 'read by the fire' day and order takeout for lunch."

"Or… we could reconstruct our island paradise and read on the beach."

"And order lunch?"

"Of course."

They both grinned. "I'll have to go home and get my suit when we're finished with breakfast."

<hr>

Peter returned to Rutherford Mansion with his deputies and knocked on the front door.

James answered and invited them in. "Any progress so far?"

Peter gave Hugh a nod before he replied. "It's early yet. I'd like to search the passage again. Mr. Taft and his date must have gone somewhere."

"I noticed there's still a car out front. Would you like some help?"

"If you can spare the time, it would make it easier."

"Hugh, are you and Sal willing to lend a hand?"

Glancing at the construction chief, Hugh nodded. "I'm starting to think we should just block off all the entrances. Having to search them time and again is annoying at best."

"I know how you feel, and I'm sorry to ask you again. I just don't know where else they could have gone without anyone seeing them."

***

They split up as they had done on their first search of the passages and thirty minutes later Peter's radio crackled. Deputy Bloom and the construction chief reported finding Mr. Taft outside the passage on the third floor.

Peter immediately telephoned Chief Lloyd and requested assistance, before making his way to the third floor. The foul smell of death, combined with his sleep deprivation, made his stomach heave. Deciding to wait for the ME, he had the others carefully accompany him out of the storage closet and closed the door. He leaned against the wall, puzzling over this latest development.

Mr. Taft was his chief suspect and now he was dead, and his date was still missing. *How did he get up here? Did she kill him? Does that mean she stabbed Mark?* Peter shook his head. *Aunt Marge is right. I need some sleep. Nothing is making sense right now.*

Chief Lloyd appeared on the third-floor landing, followed closely by the ME and the crime scene techs. "Where is he?"

Standing wearily, Peter pointed at the closet door.

"Have you slept, Locke? You look terrible."

Peter shook his head.

"Go get some sleep. I'll let you know when Starke is finished with the autopsy."

"Thank you, chief. I'm not thinking straight anymore."

"Go now. We'll talk later."

Peter didn't need to be told twice. He just hoped he could make it home in one piece.

<hr>

Waking to a ringing phone, Peter's groggy brain tried to remember what day it was. He picked up his phone and tried to hit the answer button but missed. Twice. The ringing stopped and began again. "Hullo," he mumbled.

"Good morning sleeping beauty. Time to report to the station."

"I'll be there in a few," he said to no one. Chief Lloyd had already hung up.

Rolling out of bed with a groan, Peter quickly splashed some water on his face and got dressed. He didn't need to wear his uniform as it was Sunday.

When he arrived, the team was assembled in the incident room. He poured himself a cup of viscous coffee and grabbed a donut from the side table before taking his place next to the chief.

"Thank you for coming in," Starke said. "I've completed the autopsy and wanted to explain the results, as they are slightly irregular."

Peter nodded and took a bite of his donut.

"The victim sustained multiple blows to the head, shortly after Mr. Stubbs was stabbed. No more than an hour, I'd say. A large rock with blood on it was found near his body, but there were no signs of a struggle or self-defense because he was already dead."

"What was the cause of death?" Peter asked.

"He had a massive heart attack."

"Might the perpetrator have hit him while he was in the throes of the heart attack?"

"No, there wasn't enough blood."

"Why would he hit him repeatedly after he was already dead?"

"It's your job to figure that out." Starke winked.

"Perhaps the assailant didn't realize he was dead already."

"Any other details we should know about?" The chief wiped chocolate icing off his square chin.

"The blows were forceful and made while the victim was laying on his back. They could have been made by someone very strong, or by someone fueled by adrenaline and using both hands."

Rubbing his hands over his face, Peter once again felt adrift. The results didn't appear to help at all. "Why a rock? Did he take it with him?"

Starke just shook his head.

"Was he moved?"

"No, left where he landed."

Chapter 18

Marge and Joey stopped for Millicent on the way to church and were about to climb the stairs to the entry, when Sayuri appeared in their path.

"Please, Joey," she said. "I need your help."

Joey looked at Marge who said, "Go ahead. We'll save you a seat."

He gave her an apologetic smile and walked away with Sayuri. "What is it?"

"The police suspect me of stabbing Mark, and I don't have anywhere to stay. I don't know anyone else in town. Can I please stay with you until he's well? I won't be any trouble. I promise."

He paused and looked at his feet. "Let's talk to Marge about this. We're having lunch after the service, and we'll figure something out, okay?"

She looked crestfallen and he felt a pang of guilt, but the thought of her staying in his home made him feel uncomfortable. Marge would know what to do. Walking back to the church, Joey pondered the distance that had grown between them over decades apart. He no longer knew this woman he had once been so close to.

Scooting into the pew next to Marge, he picked up a hymnal and joined in as the congregation sang 'Hark the Herald Angels Sing.' The songs and sermons leading up to Christmas always lifted his spirits.

In the vestibule after the service, they met up with their friends and walked the few blocks to the Fireside café. Marge had called ahead, so three tables were pushed together for their party of eight, and Helen greeted them as the little bell on the door announced their arrival.

"Good afternoon. Thank you for letting me know you were coming. Your table is ready, and I've left menus just in case." Helen smiled brightly, her strawberry blonde hair and freckles reminding Joey of her cousin Seth.

"What's the special today?" Joey inquired.

"Ribs and coleslaw with a side of baked beans and garlic bread."

"My mouth is watering already." James grinned.

"It sounds pretty heavy," Freida said as they were getting seated. She picked up the menu and studied it.

The little bell jangled again as Pastor Greg held the door for Harriet. Approaching the table, he pushed his square, black glasses further up on the bridge of his small nose. "Sorry we're late. One of the parishioners needed to talk."

"Don't worry. We haven't even ordered yet," Joey told him. "Does everyone know Sayuri?"

Pastor Greg, Harriet, and Millicent introduced themselves before Helen reappeared.

"Are you ready to order? Who wants the special?"

Everyone except Freida and Sayuri raised a hand. "Six specials."

Freida said, "I'd like the tuna melt and tomato soup."

Helen focused her attention on Sayuri.

"Do you have any vegetarian options?"

"You could get the grilled cheese with tomato soup? Or a salad? Cheese ravioli?"

"I'll have the grilled cheese and tomato soup. That sounds good."

"Would anyone like coffee or a drink? An appetizer?"

Everyone opted for coffee except Sayuri, who chose tea, and Helen swished away to the kitchen.

Joey cleared his throat and said, "Sayuri needs a place to stay while Mark is in the hospital. Does anyone have any suggestions?"

Marge noticed Sayuri stiffen and look down. Joey appeared slightly alarmed. "You can stay with me," she said. "I have plenty of room."

Sayuri looked up at her. "You don't mind?"

"Not at all."

"Thank you."

She thought Sayuri frowned at Joey, but it was so brief she could have been mistaken. Then she was distracted by Helen's return.

Helen passed out drinks and promised to return shortly with their food.

Joey took a sip of his coffee and turned to James. "Have the police turned up any more clues?"

"They found a body on the third floor."

Harriet gasped and Millicent gaped.

"Who was it?"

"Douglas Taft, the man who was arguing with Mark. The police were looking for him."

"Was it murder?"

"I don't know. They're keeping it under wraps. Freida's been nervous."

"I'm not sure I want to live in that house anymore."

"I'm moving home this week, if you two want to stay in my little house until the police arrest whoever's doing all this."

"Oh, Millicent! That would be wonderful. Thank you!"

"Hugh said his construction crew finally found the basement door, behind some bushes around back. He has a locksmith coming tomorrow if you want to be there."

"We'll be there." Joey looked at Marge. "Any idea what time?"

"I think he said around nine."

"After yoga then?"

Marge nodded. "You can accompany us if you'd like," she told Sayuri. "Where is your suitcase?"

"It's in Mark's car. I parked it at the church."

After lunch, Joey and Marge walked back to the church with Sayuri to collect the car, then drove to Marge's house.

"I think I'd like a little rest," Joey said. "I'll be back in a couple of hours."

"You go ahead. Maybe Sayuri and I will take our repose as well once she gets settled."

Marge helped Sayuri with her luggage and showed her to the guest room, pointing out the towels and extra sundry items in the guest bathroom. "Let me show you around downstairs, then you can make yourself at home."

She pointed out the television and where she kept the remote, then led her into the kitchen. Fluster sat in front of his bowl and stared at Marge, tapping his tail against the tile floor. "This is Fluster. He's always hungry. And this is the pantry." Marge opened the glass door and reached in for a scoop of kibble. "Help yourself to anything you like. I don't usually make tea, but the pot's in here." She opened a cupboard. "And the strainer is in here." She opened a drawer.

"Thank you, Marge. I appreciate your hospitality. I asked Joey if I could stay at his house, but..." She paused and canted her head, her shiny black bob tilting in the same direction. "He seemed very uncomfortable with that idea."

"I imagine he may feel awkward after so many years."

"Are you two..."

Marge gazed at her, wondering what her word choice might be.

"Are you... an item?"

"We're best friends." Marge grinned. "I'll rest prior to preparing our evening repast. Feel free to do the same, or unpack, watch TV, whatever you like. I'll see you shortly."

She went upstairs and into her room where she sat on the edge of her bed and took Fergus out of his cage. Holding the tiny mouse against her chest, she hoped she was doing the right thing.

As usual, Marge slept hard. This time, however, she set three alarms on her phone, one every ten minutes, so she managed to rouse herself in time to start dinner. She wasn't sure what to make for her vegetarian guest, so she made spaghetti and set aside some sauce before she added meat. Then she prepared a salad and some garlic bread and started a pot of coffee. The timer on the pasta dinged at the same time Joey knocked on the front door. Sayuri trailed him as he entered the kitchen. "Dinner is about ready. Sit wherever you like."

Sayuri sat next to Joey as Marge ferried plates to the table and sat across from them. Sayuri looked at her plate.

"Don't worry. Yours doesn't contain meat." Marge smiled.

"But mine does. You went all out, Marge. Do we have pie?"

"No, sorry. No pie today." She got up again to answer the door and found Seth waiting on the front porch.

"Something smells great."

"Come on in, you rascal." She hung his coat in the hall closet and followed him as he raced to the kitchen.

Skidding to a stop, he said, "Oh. I didn't know you had company."

"Sayuri is staying with me for a few days. Have a seat, and I'll get you a plate."

"I saw you at the bus station," Seth said, helping himself to salad. "That day it snowed, and all the lights went out."

Sayuri gazed at him with fathomless black eyes and the inscrutable expression she often wore.

Seth fidgeted. "Can I stay over tonight, Uncle Joey?"

"Yes, of course. Do you want a ride to school?"

"I have tomorrow off."

Joey nodded. "We'll be heading over to the Rutherford place in the morning so just let yourself out."

"Thanks. Your spaghetti is fire, Aunt Marge. Can I go play with Fergus?"

"Of course. Just keep an eye on Fluster."

"Thanks!" He dropped his dishes in the sink and raced out of the room."

"So much energy."

Sayuri looked from Marge to Joey.

"Honorary nephew," Marge clarified. "Would you like seconds?"

"No, thank you. It was delicious, but I'm full."

"I'll have another helping, since there's no pie." Joey chuckled and handed his plate to Marge.

Chapter 19

After yoga and a shower, Marge went downstairs and fed Fluster. She started the coffee and turned, surprised when Joey walked into the kitchen.

"Where's Sayuri?" he asked.

"She has not yet descended."

"Her car isn't in the driveway and the front door was unlocked."

"Perhaps she went to visit Mark." Marge left the kitchen and trotted up the stairs to check Sayuri's room. Opening the door and scanning the room, she was shocked to find it empty. She left the door open and slowly made her way back downstairs. "She bore her belongings. Did I cause her discomfort?"

"I can't imagine you did, but it's been thirty years since I've seen her, and I don't feel like I know her anymore."

"At least she has shelter and transportation. Perhaps she decided to stay at Mark's house after all."

The locksmith arrived at the mansion shortly after they did. She was a tall, stout woman of indeterminate age, wearing coveralls and a toolbelt sprouting tools of every shape and size imaginable. She carried a large toolbox which, when she opened it, showed a plethora of keys and locks. Hugh consulted with her for a few minutes, before instructing her to remove the lock on the door and replace it with another. Then he stood back with James and Freida as she got to work.

She succeeded in removing the lock, and the door swung open. "You can go in now if you want. I'll get the new lock installed." She stood back and let them pass.

Bumping and jostling occurred as the five of them looked around in awe, alternately stopping and running into each other.

The basement, which ran underneath the entire length and breadth of the house, was made exclusively of stone. The main room was large and open, with archways leading into a perimeter of smaller rooms. Small vents and camouflaged windows were set high in the walls and joined by battery and gas-powered lamps and space heaters for light, heat, and ventilation.

"I see now where some of the household items went," Hugh said, running his hand along the back of an antique sofa and examining the area rugs. "It smells like paint down here."

Walking from room to room, they found two sleeping quarters, a room set up like a studio full of paintings, and a natural, underground spring which had been made into a bubbling pool.

Marge crouched and stuck a hand in the pool. "I read about this spring in the journal. It's warm."

One room, apparently used for storage, had a wooden door on one end, with a padlock holding it closed. Hugh knocked on the door and received a knock in reply. "Is that you, Deputy Bloom?"

"Yes, sir. Mr. Rutherford?" Deputy Dennis Bloom's voice sounded muffled from the other side.

"Yes, we'll see about removing this lock from the inside." Hugh left to find the locksmith, who followed him to the interior door and received further instructions.

The little group found a staircase in a room that served as a kitchen. It led to another door without a visible catch. Hugh climbed the stairs two at a time and felt around the edges with his fingertips. The door slowly swung open to reveal the first-floor kitchen.

"Behold, the ghostly passage," Marge said dramatically, joining Hugh at the top and peering around him into the kitchen.

Freida gasped.

"One mystery solved," Joey added from below.

"I wonder how it opens from the other side. Stay here and let me watch it close," Marge said.

She and Hugh experimented with the door until they figured out the trick, then Hugh instructed the locksmith to place a lock on that exit as well.

Finally, they found a room which opened into a tunnel leading away from the house.

"I wonder where this leads," Hugh said. "I'd like Sergeant Locke to be here when we investigate."

Marge left the tunnel entrance and returned to the room full of paintings. Joey was right behind her. She bent and looked at the signatures on the paintings. "Nicole Reid."

"Who's that?"

"She must be our midnight ghost. She painted that picture in Millicent's living room, the blue and green one. How strange." She paused and stared at the paintings.

The locksmith declared her work was done and Hugh walked her outside, then reentered a few minutes later, followed by Mr. Taft's date, Nicky, and Deputy Bloom, who had been lurking outside. Nicky, who looked no more than twenty-five, removed her hat, releasing waist-length, silver hair.

"Nicole Reid, I presume. These are your work?" Marge asked.

Nicole nodded silently.

"They're stunning."

Staring at her paintings, a tear rolled down her cheek.

"This is a pretty nice setup you have here. Who lives with you?" Hugh asked. His question was met with a defiant stare, so he shrugged. "Since this is my house, I have changed the locks, but you can have the key and stay here for now." He handed her a key, which she accepted. "The entrance to the secret passages and the entrance to the kitchen have been locked, since we can't have strangers wandering about the house, but again, you are welcome to stay."

"Thank you," she whispered, looking at her feet.

"Come around to the front door if you need anything."

He asked Deputy Bloom to arrange a meeting with Peter and left the basement with James and Freida.

Marge and Joey followed, Marge glancing back at Nicole. She leaned toward Joey and whispered, "I wonder what provoked her tears when I admired her paintings."

Marge and Joey were lounging in the sitting room with James and Freida when Peter joined them. The roaring fire felt good after the cold outside and his stomach rumbled when he spied two plates full of sandwiches on the coffee table.

"Help yourself," Freida said. "Would you like some coffee?"

"Yes, please; if it's no trouble."

She picked up a silver pot and poured him a cup. "I brought it in so we wouldn't have to run back and forth."

"Do you have any updates?" Joey asked.

"I placed a couple of listening devices in the basement and left Bloom behind the basement door, so we can hear what happens when Ms. Reid's roommate returns. Now, we wait." Peter set a small receiver on the table.

"You're being awfully quiet, Aunt Marge."

Marge gazed at him and blinked. "Isn't she wanted for questioning regarding the stabbing and death that occurred during the party?"

"Yes. I still want to interview her, but if I take her in now, we won't find out about her roommate."

The receiver crackled and came to life and an angry male voice said, "Why did you let those people in here?"

"I didn't. They were already in here when I got back."

"How did they get in, then?"

"They had a locksmith. She changed the locks, but the owner gave me a key and said I could stay."

"What did he want in return? What did you tell him?"

"Nothing. I didn't say anything. I swear."

"Lying cow. You're going to ruin everything. Get your coat."

"I don't want to go out there. It's so cold."

"Get your coat or it'll be colder. Put some long johns on too. You'll need them."

The group in the sitting room heard rustling sounds and then, "Hurry up!"

"I'm trying."

"Come on! You first."

The woman cried out once and some swearing ensued, then silence. Marge looked unusually pale. "We must go after them."

"It's dark, and they'll have gone through the tunnel. I think we'll need to wait until morning," James said.

"No, we can't postpone. Ms. Reid could be in danger." Peter radioed for backup and went downstairs to confer with deputy Bloom.

Chapter 20

They were all waiting outside when Peter's backup arrived. Sergeant Dawson approached and said, "Locke, this is Sergeant Tanya Holmes from the Chesterville station."

"Glad to have your assistance, Sergeant." Peter glanced down nervously as her canine partner growled deep in his throat.

"Don't mind Surge. He's very well trained." She shook Peter's hand, her firm grip surprising him.

Marge approached him as he was positioning his headlamp. "James and I could provide additional backup. He's very strong."

"Absolutely not. We don't know if the perpetrator is armed. You stay here and wait."

"But—"

"No, Aunt Marge." He glared at her.

"So stubborn," Marge mumbled.

"Let's go," Peter said, joining Fred and Tanya inside the tunnel entrance. "You and Surge can take the lead."

<hr>

Although they walked softly, the sound of their boots echoed through the otherwise silent stone tunnel. After what seemed like miles, the tunnel curved and began to decrease in size.

Halting before a wall with four stone steps and a person-sized hole at the top, Tanya said, "Could one of you see what's through there? I don't want to send Surge through without knowing if it's safe. He doesn't have the same self-preservation instincts that we do."

"I'll go," Peter said. He climbed the steps and put his torso through the hole before disappearing on the other side.

Presently, his head popped through the hole. "You can come through. We've reached the end of the tunnel."

Once they had all climbed through the exit and pushed through the camouflaging bushes, they extinguished their headlamps and quietly scanned their environment.

Pulling out a blouse she had found in the basement, Tanya allowed Surge to smell it. He snuffled it for a moment, then sniffed the air before following his nose in widening circles through the brush. Finally, he looked up at his handler and wagged his tail twice before pulling intently on his lead.

Tanya made a hand signal to follow him. They walked as quietly as they could through the dry leaves and brush, but Peter surmised that they sounded like a herd of elephants to the occupants of the forest.

"Try to remember where that tunnel entrance is," Peter whispered to Dawson as they hurried to keep up.

Zigzagging this way and that, Surge finally stopped in front of the ruins of a stone hut and braced all four legs near the ground, a deep growl emanating from his chest. Sergeant Holmes signaled for Peter and Fred to check either side of the building and pulled out her gun before releasing Surge and flipping on her headlamp.

Peter sprinted around the ruin, entering the back as Tanya entered the front. In the center of the hut sat Nicole Reid, slumped to the side, unconscious. She was tied to a metal folding chair, duct tape across her mouth.

Surge sat quietly as his handler approached Nicole. She asked Peter to pull the skin on one side of Nicole's mouth taught, and she held the other as she quickly ripped the tape away, then she began working on the rope.

"We need to get her medical attention and call for backup. Do you have any idea where we are?"

"Yes, but it's quite a distance from the house."

Surge stood and began to growl, his ears lying flat.

Dawson looked in through the front entrance. "Someone's coming."

Peter went outside with him as Joey pulled up in front of the hut in his UTV. He switched off the ignition and rolled down the window. "I thought you might be here. Do you need a ride?"

"Yes, actually. Ms. Reid needs medical assistance. I thought I told you to stay put."

"Technically, you told us not to follow you into the tunnel."

"Where's Aunt Marge?"

"She and James followed you into the tunnel." Joey chuckled.

Peter rolled his eyes. "Let's figure out how to transport Ms. Reid without further injuring her."

Leaving Joey in the UTV, Peter reentered the hut to find Tanya laying Nicole on her side on the floor, before cutting the last of the rope.

"I didn't want her to fall," she explained.

"Thank you, Sergeant. Would you mind staying with Surge and Dawson until further backup arrives? Mr. Cattywampus has arrived in his offroad vehicle, but it's a two-seater. We can transport Ms. Reid back to the house and lead the others here when they arrive."

"I don't mind, but you could bring me back a hot cup of coffee if you like."

Seeing her smile for the first time, Peter's pulse fluttered unexpectedly. "I'll see what I can do." He gave his head a shake as he walked away. *No, no, no. That would be very awkward.*

He found Dawson around back. "Did you call it in?"

"Yes, sir."

"Could you help me get Ms. Reid into the UTV? I'm going to ride back with Mr. Cattywampus. I'd like you to stay here with Sergeant Holmes until I return."

"Yes, sir."

They went back inside the hut and gently lifted Nicole, carrying her to the UTV.

Peter got inside and Fred helped set her on his lap. "I'll be back as soon as reinforcements arrive."

Joey backed up and drove toward the mansion, where flashing lights could be seen in the distance.

⁂

Extending a hand, James helped Marge out of the tunnel exit, then stood with her, scanning the woods. "Look at those bobbing lights," she said. "They must be over there." She pulled a flashlight out of her coat pocket and struggled to turn it on without removing her gloves.

"Maybe we shouldn't turn on our flashlights until we find out what's happening. The moon is bright."

Marge returned her flashlight to her pocket and took two steps before tripping on a root. "Oof." James caught her before she hit the ground.

"Watch your feet," he whispered.

It occurred to Marge, as they stumbled through the overgrowth, that they might be less obvious if they had used flashlights.

The bobbing lights got closer, and she heard a low growl. "James." She stinkered twice.

He heard the toots, stopped, and turned, bracing for impact. He grabbed Marge's shoulders when she ran into him. "What is it?"

"Do coyotes growl?"

"I don't know."

"Something growled nearby."

"Maybe it's the police dog."

"Let's hurry."

"Okay. Turn your flashlight on. They'll know we're here anyway."

Tanya and Surge met them as they approached the hut. "Halt! Identify yourselves."

"James Nelson and Marge Bumfuzzle, Sergeant Locke's aunt."

"Oh, for heaven's sake. What are you doing out here?"

"I'm sorry, Sergeant Holmes, is it? We thought you might need assistance."

"Sergeant Locke has taken the victim back to the house and will be returning with backup shortly."

"How did he transport her to the mansion? We didn't see him."

Your friend drove here in a small offroad vehicle.

"Joey cheated," Marge said, and James grinned.

"Maybe he can give you a ride back after he drops off Sergeant Locke, or you could go back the way you came."

"We'll wait." She looked around. "Did they leave you here by yourself?"

"No, Sergeant Dawson is here with me, and Surge of course. Could you possibly stand by this wall until they get back? I'm meant to be on patrol, but the perpetrator might be nearby, and I don't want you to get hurt."

"We could help. James is very strong, and we have flashlights."

"No, really, if you could just stay here so I can do my job, that would be great."

Marge sighed. "As you wish." She glanced at James.

"No, Marge," he whispered as Tanya walked away. "Just stay put. Look. I think that's Joey."

Marge craned her neck as Joey approached in the UTV, the lights bouncing around in the trees as it bumped over obstacles on the forest floor. Two officers jumped out of the back as he pulled to a stop, and Peter opened the front passenger door. He spoke to Joey before turning to find Marge and James standing in front of him. "Unbelievable. You can't ever listen, can you?"

"You already knew we were here because we weren't at the house. Sergeant Holmes said Joey could give us a ride back."

"Fine with me. Just don't let the chief see you out here." He turned and left them with a frown.

"Only room for one I'm afraid," Joey said when Marge opened the passenger door. "You'll have to get in the back, Marge."

"Heyy."

He chuckled. "You know I'm just kidding. I'm sure James doesn't mind too much."

"Of course not." James grinned. "I'm weatherproof."

"I believe it, too. He's like Superman. I won't ever worry about Freida again." Marge got in the cab. "It's getting late."

"Maybe we'd better get some sleep and let the police do their jobs. At least we know that young lady is safe, and the house is secure."

When Joey parked, they all got out of the UTV and went to find Freida. She was in the sitting room with Paws and looked up when they entered. "Are you taking the day off, James?"

"Yes. I'll need to stay up until the police give the all-clear."

"We should probably get home. Do we have any of those sandwiches left?"

"Yes, I put them in the refrigerator. Can't we get some sleep, James? They have an officer in the basement and another outside, and it will be light soon."

"Maybe you're right. Let me check in with them. Joey, Marge, you two officially have tomorrow off, unless you want to come check on the investigation."

"We may take you up on that since it's already tomorrow." Joey looked at his watch. "Come on Marge. Grab a couple of sandwiches and let's head home.

Chapter 21

When Marge woke, she was once again unsure of the date. She had finally crawled into bed on Wednesday morning as the sun began to rise, and it was shining brightly in her window when she opened her eyes. Her clock read ten o'clock. *That can't be right.* She sat up and looked at her phone. *Thursday? Where did Wednesday go?* She texted Joey. "Are you awake?"

"I've been awake and asleep again. I thought maybe you ate the poisoned apple," he texted back. "Are you ready for breakfast?"

"Yes! I'm famished."

"I'll be there in five minutes."

True to his word, he was at her door before she finished getting dressed.

Letting him in, she said, "I lost an entire day."

"So you did, but I bet you feel better."

"What kept you occupied while I was slumbering?"

"I read a little bit and checked in with James and Peter. Would you like to go to the Fireside café?"

"No, I can make breakfast. What would you like?"

"Whatever you want."

Marge put bacon in a pan and began to crack eggs. "We so rarely dine at home. Everything is going to spoil. Have you heard from Sayuri?"

Joey started a pot of coffee and put some bread in the toaster. "Not a peep."

"I believe she purloined my copy of the journal, but I am unable to deduce the reason." Marge frowned.

"You can have my copy."

"Did anything interesting transpire while I was sleeping?"

"Ms. Reid is in the hospital and still refusing to talk other than to express worry about her paintings, so James and Freida moved them into the house."

"I imagine they are worth a lot of money. I wonder why she hasn't sold them." Marge dished out the food and poured coffee, ferrying them to the table before sitting across from Joey. "Are we expected at the mansion today?"

"Nope. We have the day off."

"Why don't we make a fire and enjoy the tree. I can put on some Christmas music a-a-and-" she paused dramatically, "I have cookies and cocoa."

"I can go get the book I've been reading and the journal."

"You could assist with wrapping as well. That way you'll know what we got for everyone." She grinned.

"I was there when you bought them."

"You were, but I'll wager you don't recall who receives what."

Joey chuckled. "You would win."

<hr>

They sat on the floor, in front of the fireplace, listening to Christmas music and wrapping presents. The tree glowed in the corner, and Marge was filled with a deep sense of contentment. Christmas was her favorite time of year. Joey hummed along with the music, stopping now and then to inquire about a gift. Even Fluster had joined them and was purring on the back of the sofa.

Holding up a red, metal device with a rotating handle and a corkscrew rod, Joey asked, "What's this?"

"That's an apple peeler for Harriet. You know how she loves apple pie."

Joey turned it over, examining each side. "How's it work?"

"Come in the kitchen. I have one too." Marge rose and led Joey into the kitchen. Taking an apple from the fridge, she pulled out her peeler and stuck the apple on the end. "Now turn the handle."

Joey's eyes widened as he watched the device peel the apple and remove the core. "Whoever came up with this is brilliant."

"Indeed. Are you ready for cookies, or should we have lunch first?"

"Such a silly question."

Marge grabbed a plate of assorted cookies and carried them into the living room. "I believe our wrapping is nearly complete."

"I can't say I'm not glad. Wrapping one gift isn't bad, but we have so many."

"When Petey was little, I used to prepare a stocking from Santa, wrapping each tiny toy separately to make it more fun. Matchbox cars, pencil sets, chocolate coins, socks. By the time I finished, the wrapping became somewhat haphazard." Marge laughed, remembering the chore of wrapping made worthwhile by her young nephew's excitement on Christmas morning. She finished the gift she was working on and set it down. "Done."

Joey sat his down next to it. "Done. Let's make that cocoa."

⎯⎯⎯⎯⎯ ⟶∽⟵ ⎯⎯⎯⎯⎯

Full of cookies and cocoa, Joey dozed off in his recliner while Marge continued to read the journal with fascination. Abraham Rutherford must have been a very interesting person, she thought, and his journal entries captured her imagination.

> *8.April.1903*
> *Since my sweet Edith is on bedrest and unable to enjoy the*
> *gardens with any frequency, I have decided to surprise her with*
> *a secret garden where she can experience quiet relaxation.*
> *Hidden away, with a small pond and lush foliage, the garden*
> *will be her own magical place of solitude.*

That must be the garden beyond the patio. The same place he met Anabelle twelve years later. It must have been glorious.

She closed her eyes and tried to picture what that garden must have looked like until, lulled by the warm crackle of the fire, she fell asleep.

She dreamt of an elegant lady in long skirts and a bonnet carrying a tiny baby wrapped in a fuzzy blanket. By her side, a gentleman with side whiskers and wearing a mourning coat gazed lovingly at her as they strolled beneath weeping willow trees.

Suddenly, the man turned into Joey, and he said, "Marge, wake up."

The woman with the baby said, "Who are you talking to, Abraham?"

"Marge. Peter's here." She felt a hand on her shoulder and her eyes blinked open.

"Sorry, Aunt Marge." Peter stood near the door with his cap in his hands. "I told him not to wake you. I just wanted to invite you to dinner."

"What time is it?" She yawned.

"It's almost six. I just got off."

"We didn't have lunch. What do you think, Joey?"

"I think you won't have to make dinner if we eat out."

Chapter 22

When they arrived at Rutherford Mansion the following day, Marge waved hello to Freida and made a beeline for the side patio where the magical garden lay. She walked among the overgrowth, picturing the garden as it once was. The path, although barely discernible, peeked through at intervals. Ornate benches hid among the branches of large willow trees and untrimmed shrubbery. A ray of sunlight appeared from behind a dark cloud and reflected on a shiny object resting on the branch of a particularly bushy plant.

Unable to reach it with her hand, Marge attempted to climb over the plant. She bent her right knee and lifted her leg as high as she could, before swinging it toward the far side of the plant, then when she found herself straddling the bush and unable to move, she swung her left leg over to follow the right. The branches bowed under her weight as she attempted to slide down the other side.

Unfortunately, her right foot landed on a slippery surface, propelling her forward. "Augh," she hollered, before she went under.

The pond wasn't deep; once Marge sat up, it only reached her shoulders. But it was disgusting.

Murky green and smelling of decay, long strands of moss and mottled orange and black fish moved around in the dark, fetid water. The air outside was cold, and the water near freezing. She knew she needed to get out immediately, but the bottom was too slick to walk on. Holding her breath and sealing her mouth shut, she rolled over and doggy paddled to the side, where she could grab an overhanging branch. She grabbed the branch and pulled, but it broke, landing her back in the pond.

She wanted to cry. *One more time.*

She swam toward the edge again and grabbed several branches with each hand, as high up as she could. Her body was heavy with water-logged clothing and her muscles screamed, but little by little she pulled herself out of the pond and over the bush. She lay on the ground panting for several minutes, until Paws stood over her and licked her face.

Joey, unable to navigate the overgrowth of the garden, was drawn to the entrance of what looked like the remains of a hedgerow maze. He wandered for a long time; wrong turns leading to dead ends or winding in circles. At least the path is even, and the hedges break the wind. I wonder what Marge is up to.

He looked up at the overcast sky, above the soaring hedges. It occurred to him that he should have somehow marked the trail so he could find his way out, but it was too late for that.

Finally, he arrived at an ornate but currently dry fountain at what he assumed was the center of the maze. He thought he saw a figure sitting on the ground with his back against the base. The air was very still and the silence pervasive.

Slowly approaching the fountain and calling out softly to avoid startling the person sitting there, he suddenly perceived a slight movement behind him. In a fraction of a second, his training kicked in, and he instinctively turned in a crouch with his elbows out. Bending his head down and extending his arms, he grabbed his assailant's arm, effectively stopping the forward momentum of the hammer he held.

Joey's swift response and training prevented him from receiving a possibly lethal blow, but his lack of balance landed him and his assailant on the ground. He grabbed the hammer, but his attacker rolled away from him and jumped to his feet.

At the sound of Marge's voice, they both glanced toward the entrance.

"Hush, Paws. It's just me," he heard Marge say. "Joo-ee-y," she called.

When his focus shifted back to his attacker, he saw him sprint toward the wall of shrubs on the opposite side of the clearing and disappear.

Paws arrived first, followed by Marge, dripping and trailing vines in an excellent impression of a sea monster. "What are you doing down there?" she asked, shivering violently, and reaching out a green hand to help him up.

He knew what was coming and shook his head with a smile. He didn't want to land on her, so he turned to get on his knees. "Perhaps you could just bring my walker over here."

Once he was on his feet, he took off his coat and placed it around her shoulders before moving slowly toward the figure by the fountain.

Marge, right behind him, leaned over his shoulder. Her teeth had begun to chatter.

Joey threw his walker aside and knelt to check for a pulse. "Call an ambulance," he said urgently. "She's still alive, but just barely."

"Let me have yours. Mine doesn't work anymore." After calling 9-1-1 and Peter, she silently knelt beside Joey. He felt her presence but reeling from shock at seeing Sayuri so near death, his words stuck in his throat.

⁂

Paws led Peter and the first responders into the clearing, interrupting their vigil. After Sayuri was lifted onto a gurney and whisked away to the hospital, Peter approached Marge and Joey. He handed Marge a blanket one of the first responders had given him. "What happened here? Are you both okay?"

Joey saw Peter eyeing his aunt and admired his restraint. He and Marge related what had happened. "He somehow exited over there." Joey pointed.

"What's with the hammer?"

"He tried to hit me with it."

Peter's eyes widened slightly. "You disarmed him?"

Joey nodded.

"We'd better bag it as evidence." He pulled out a large plastic bag and had Joey drop the hammer inside, then walked toward the wall of soaring shrubs where Joey had indicated. Joey and Marge followed, and the three of them poked at the wall.

It was Paws who showed them the camouflaged exit. He barked, wagged his tail, and pushed through the partial opening. Following his lead, Peter, Joey, and Marge pushed through as well, finding themselves on a path that looked like all the others within the maze.

Swiveling his head in both directions, Peter began pushing at the shrubs again before Paws, still wagging his tail, led them to the second exit. The fourth led to the edge of the woods.

"Someone put a lot of effort into their escape hatch. What did your attacker look like, Joey?"

"He looked a lot like the self-proclaimed caretaker, but I don't think it was him."

"Why not?"

"I'm not sure." He wrinkled his brow. "His facial expressions were different. The caretaker threatened us with a gun and watched us leave with a scowl but..." Joey shook his head. "Something was different."

Peter looked thoughtful. "How likely is it that we have twin loons wandering the property?"

"I didn't say they were twins, just that there was a similarity. I've only seen the caretaker once and could be completely wrong."

Peter sighed. "Did you recognize the victim?"

"Yes, I guess you did too."

"I wonder what she was doing out here."

Chapter 23

Joey bundled Marge into the UTV and cranked up the heat. *She'll have hypothermia if she's not careful.* "Did you secure the item you were after in the garden?"

"Yes." She held out her hand, still clutching a wedding ring. "It doesn't look very old."

Joey didn't feel entirely convinced that the ring was worth getting soaked in smelly water, but he didn't mention that. He parked his UTV in front of Marge's house and looked over at her. "I'm exhausted."

"So am I. It must be cumulative."

"Why don't we order take out and make it an early night?"

Marge shivered. "I don't wish to exit your vehicle. I can't seem to thaw."

"Would you like me to go inside and light a fire while you call?"

"What shall we eat? Chinese?"

"Sure. Order a lot. I'm starving." Joey battled the several yards of icy wind and let himself in through Marge's front door. After building the fire, he got into the UTV and said, "Are you ready? Marge?"

She snored softly, making him chuckle. "Marge." He tapped her shoulder. "Marge, the fire's lit. Did you call the restaurant?"

"Yes." Her eyes popped open. "Did I fall asleep?"

"You did. Are you ready to go inside?"

"No, but I suppose we must."

Joey turned off the ignition and they both got out of the UTV and went inside. "I think it might snow again. That wind is frigid."

"Why don't you take a hot shower and change into something dry, then you can sit by the fire. I started the coffee too."

Marge had to be prodded a bit, but she finally stumbled upstairs.

⸺⸺⸺ ·⸱�⊰⊱⸱· ⸺⸺⸺

Joey answered a knock at the door and said, "That was quick," as he opened it. "Seth. Come on in. I thought you were the delivery driver. How have you been?" Before Seth could answer, there was another knock. Opening the door, a second time, Joey was surprised to see Peter on the front step. He motioned him inside. "Marge is upstairs getting cleaned up. We're expecting Chinese food if you'd like to join us."

"Only if you have enough," Peter said at the same time Seth said, "I love Chinese food!"

"Come on in the kitchen for a hot drink. Would you like cocoa, Seth?"

The delivery driver arrived shortly before Marge reappeared and, based on the number of bags he'd been given, Joey figured she had ordered plenty.

"When did you two get here?" Marge asked when she entered the kitchen.

"They got here a few minutes ago. What all did you order?"

"I got rice, fried rice, noodles, and one of each kind of chicken. It looks like plenty." Marge pulled paper plates and plastic utensils from the pantry and poured coffee for Joey, Peter, and herself. "What would you like to drink, Seth?"

"Water is fine. I can get it. Why are you…?"

"I was wet and green. It's a long story."

Once they were all seated and had dished out their food, Marge said, "How is Sayuri doing?"

"She has a concussion. I went to interview her, but she's asking for Joey. Can you come with me to the hospital after dinner?"

"Sure." Joey turned to look at Seth. "Will you be staying over?"

"No, I just wanted to stop by and say hello. I've missed you."

Joey smiled. "I've missed you too. Do you need a ride home?"

"Is that your UTV outside?"

"It is, and I have to move it anyway."

"Then, yes, I'll take a ride. It looks cool."

"Will you be alright, Marge?"

"Oh, yes. I'll just enjoy the fire for a while and then go to bed early."

Joey nodded as he stood. "Yoga tomorrow?"

"Yes, but we should perhaps begin slightly earlier than is customary, so we are able to meet Freida and James at nine."

She saw them off and sat in the living room, dozing in front of the fire.

———————※———————

Joey dropped Seth off at home and met Peter at the hospital. After checking in with the on-call doctor, Peter led the way to Sayuri's room and knocked on the door before pushing it open. "I've brought Joey as promised," Peter told her.

"Thank you." She lay with her bed in the raised position, wearing a hospital gown and a white bandage around her head.

Still wearing makeup, the black of her hair and her shiny red lips contrasted with the white all around her, reminding Joey of a glamorous actress in a hospital scene. "I would have come to visit anyway, but why did you want me here?"

"The Sergeant has questions about what happened, and I want you to know too. I never got to tell you why I came here, and you deserve an explanation." She turned to Peter. "Where would you like me to start?"

"Start at the beginning, and I'll ask questions if I need to."

Taking a deep breath, Sayuri began. "My husband, as I told you, is business partners with Mark Stubbs. He's also a crook. He embezzled the company funds and took all our savings and disappeared. He left both of us in a very bad spot."

Peter scribbled furiously in his notebook.

"I came here to talk to Mark and figure out what we should do, but when I realized that Joey lived here, I thought maybe he would help me." She gazed at Joey. "What I didn't realize was how much you've changed. You're not the same person you were when we split; you're strong and confident and surrounded by friends who really care about you." She looked down at her hands in her lap. "I thought it would be easy. You'd be happy to have me stay with you and offer me money when you found out about my situation."

Joey sat silently, listening to what she was saying and all that she wasn't. He was glad he wasn't the same person, and he wished Marge was here with him. No, perhaps Marge doesn't need to know how broken I was, how I begged.

"Continue please," Peter said.

"I was staying at Marge's house and couldn't sleep, so I wandered around looking at her things. I found a copy of a journal and started reading it. I read about a treasure. I thought if I found it, it might help Mark and me get out of our bind. So, I read some more and decided I needed to look around the basement. I waited until no one was around and snuck in."

"How did you get in?"

"The journal has instructions for entering the house through a tunnel. I drove to the opposite side of the property and located the tunnel. Unfortunately, it took a lot longer than I thought it would."

"So, you entered the basement and began to search. What were you looking for?"

"I didn't know what I was looking for. I was just poking around."

"Did you find anything?"

"No. I don't know what happened, but someone must have snuck up behind me and hit me in the head. All I remember is my head exploding then everything went dark."

"You have no idea who hit you?"

Sayuri shook her head gingerly. "None at all."

"What were you looking at when you got knocked out?"

"I was in the studio, looking at paintings."

Peter closed his notebook and stood. "I think that's all for now. Thank you for your cooperation."

"Thank you, Sergeant. And Joey? I'm sorry. For everything."

Parting ways with Joey, Peter went home for a short break. He wanted to interview Mark Stubbs, but it was getting late, and he hadn't been getting much sleep. Thinking of his aunt, he decided a shower would not be remiss, so he warmed up in a hot shower and pulled on a pair of flannel pajamas. He was asleep almost as soon as his head hit the pillow.

The following morning, feeling refreshed, he pulled his cruiser into a curb-side slot in front of Home Finder Real Estate and strode to the glass-fronted office. The door was locked, but he had an appointment, so he knocked on the glass and peered inside. It took a few moments, but Mark Stubbs finally opened the door.

"Hello, Sergeant. Sorry to keep you waiting." He drew delicate fingers along the sides of his triangular goatee. "Come on back to my office. Would you like some coffee?" He led the way with mincing steps.

Peter wondered if his shoes were too small. "Yes, I'll have a cup, thank you." Mark appeared agitated, and Peter hoped the coffee might lend a friendly, social atmosphere to the interview.

Mark invited Peter to have a seat at the coffee table and placed a cup of Keurig coffee in front of him, making another for himself, before sitting across from him and adjusting the collar of his starched, lavender shirt.

"You seem to be recovering well."

"Yes, thank you. I was released yesterday. What can I do for you, Sergeant?" He carefully picked up his coffee and took a sip.

"I would like to speak with you about Rutherford Mansion."

"Rutherford?" Mark's eyebrows rose a fraction.

"Yes, I understand you were representing Mr. Taft in his attempt to purchase the estate and that you tried to bribe the construction crew to leave their project for a more lucrative one in Chesterville."

Running a shaky hand through his gleaming black hair, Mark smiled weakly. "You don't pull any punches, do you?"

"What I would like to know is how badly you and Mr. Taft wanted the land. What was it worth to you?"

"I won't lie, Sergeant. The money I could have made from that deal would've helped me out of a tight spot."

"How tight?"

"My partner racked up a large debt, then left me holding the bag. I could lose everything." He studied a large gold ring on his middle finger, then looked up. "I thought Douglas was the answer to my prayers."

"But then Hugh Rutherford decided to renovate and rent to your daughter. Was Mr. Taft angry?"

Mark fidgeted with the cuffs of his suit jacket. "He wanted that property badly."

Peter folded his hands and leaned forward. "Would either of you have felt strongly enough about it to physically hurt someone?"

"What? No! What do you mean?"

"Did Mr. Taft threaten you at the party?"

"Not really. He told me he was disappointed in me and would be using a different realtor in the future."

"Had you met his friend, Nicky, before?"

"No. He introduced her as a client."

"And what is your connection to Sayuri Cattywampus?"

"Her last name isn't Cattywampus. She remarried. Her current husband, Chris O'Donnell, is my thieving ex-partner. He left both of us holding the bag, so to speak. We're trying to find him and doing some damage control in the meantime."

"What did she want from Mr. Cattywampus?"

"Money of course." Mark's eyebrows rose a little.

"Do you know Mr. O'Donnell's current whereabouts?"

"No, we haven't found him yet."

"Would he have any reason to harm his wife?"

"That depends. She has evidence of his criminal activity. I suppose he knows that."

"Do you know were Sayuri is now?"

Mark shook his head. "She's supposed to be here this morning. She told me she has a plan. She should be here unless she somehow talked Joey into letting her stay with him."

Carefully studying his face, Peter felt inclined to believe him. "She's in the hospital. She was found badly injured at the Rutherford place yesterday afternoon."

Mark's face grew pale. "Will she be alright?"

"Yes. I imagine they'll release her later today." Peter paused. "Could you tell me again what happened at the party? I read the report, but I'd like to hear it from you."

"Well, as I said, Douglas was angry because I hadn't managed to help him buy the Rutherford place, and I was trying to explain why I couldn't. His date was looking over my shoulder and suddenly grabbed his wrist, then the lights went out. I heard someone move behind me, so I turned and felt like someone punched me—hard. I landed on my back and couldn't get up. The next thing I knew, the lights were back on, and a crowd of people were standing around."

"Can you remember anyone specifically?"

Mark's eyes rolled up and to the right as he thought back. "Sayuri was kneeling next to me… I'm not sure."

"Do you think the assailant might have stabbed you by mistake?"

Mark shook his head. "I just don't know. Where did Douglas go?"

"We found his body on the third floor."

"So maybe they *were* after him."

"Perhaps. Do you have any idea who 'they' might be?"

Mark slowly shook his head. "I don't really know anything about him, other than our own transactions."

Peter stood and handed Mark a business card with his number printed on the back. "Thank you for your cooperation. Please call me if you remember anything else."

Accepting the card, Mark led Peter back to the front entrance and watched him return to his cruiser.

Chapter 24

Everyone congregated at the mansion to help with the continued renovation of the second-floor bedrooms. Piles of home cooked food were arranged on the kitchen table, available for anyone needing a break.

Peter was there when Marge and Joey arrived.

"Petey!" Marge smiled when she saw him in the doorway.

"Did you get caught up on your sleep?"

"I am feeling much improved. Do you have any updates?"

"Not much, I'm afraid. Why don't we sit in the kitchen and have some coffee while we talk?"

Marge nodded and motioned to Joey, before they followed Peter out of the foyer.

When they were seated, Marge asked, "How is the investigation proceeding?"

Peter shook his head.

"Have you discovered any additional clues?" Marge asked.

"Well, I believe you were right about the alcove, because Mark said he heard something behind him and turned around. Nicole doesn't appear to have a motive for killing Douglas, but she does know about the secret passages."

"Didn't he die of a heart attack?" Joey asked.

"Yes, but then someone tried to kill him after the fact."

Marge looked thoughtful.

"We still haven't found the supposed caretaker, so I ran a search for missing and wanted persons in the area and found one person of interest, a man named Gary Marshall who escaped from prison about five years ago."

"Why do you consider him of interest?" Joey asked.

"Mainly because he has family here. He has a wife named Nicole and his brother owns a pub on the outskirts of town." He looked at a piece of paper. "The brother's name is Lawrence, and his pub is called The Dark Horse. Have you heard of it?"

"Isn't that the one where bikers congregate?"

"Yeah. We usually answer calls out there on weekends."

Marge glanced at Joey. "Do you think Nicole Reid is Gary's wife?"

"It's a pretty big coincidence if she's not."

"Do you think Gary is the caretaker?"

"It would make sense, wouldn't it? We can check his fingerprints when we find him."

"Joey and I could…"

"No, Aunt Marge."

"You don't even know what I was about to say."

"It doesn't matter. You need to stay out of this investigation."

"But…"

"It could be dangerous and if the chief found out, I could lose my job. Just stay out of it."

Marge was disappointed. She had an excellent idea. *So unreasonable. I'll just wait until he leaves, then I'll tell Joey.* "Well, I guess I'll go find Freida then." She stood and left the room.

Peter and Joey watched her leave, then looked at each other; Peter with raised eyebrows and Joey with an answering shrug. "It would be so much easier if she could just act like a normal aunt."

"That would be boring," Joey retorted. "Her curiosity is part of what makes her interesting. Plus, she helped you solve Reginald's murder."

Peter blushed. "The chief thinks that was just luck."

"Well, it wasn't. She had the same clues as everyone else, and she figured it out. You should give her some credit."

"She's going to get hurt and get me fired in the meantime."

Joey rose. "Thanks for the update. I think I'll see what she's up to." He left the room and joined Marge upstairs. "What's your plan?" he asked.

"We'll visit The Dark Horse tonight. Do you suppose they have food?"

"I don't know. I could ask around. Maybe James would know. What if someone asks why we're there?"

"We could be returning from a day out and feeling cold and in need of a warming drink."

"Yes. Simple is best. I feel like I could use a warming drink right now." He smiled mischievously. "Let's see what else needs to be done, shall we?"

———————————⚬———————————

The afternoon passed quickly, and Marge was surprised when she wandered around the second floor to find it empty, apart from Joey and herself. "Where did everyone go?"

Joey looked up and shrugged. "We can finish what we're working on and go find out."

They went downstairs, but the house seemed deserted. "How curious." Moving to the large windows flanking the front entrance, Marge gasped. "Joey, come look at this."

He moved beside her, and his eyes widened. "Now when did that happen?"

Freida descended the stairs and said, "Are you two still here? We thought everyone had left because of the snow."

"The UTV should be able to handle the snow, but we were surprised. We must have a couple of feet out there."

"It started around lunch time and came down hard. People started making noises about getting home, so we called it a day."

"Joey? Where is the UTV? I don't see it."

Joey looked out the window. "The camouflage must be working very well. I'll go check." He bundled up and took one step from the door before sinking almost to his knee and saying, "Nope. Help me get turned around, please. This is something I didn't consider."

Marge waded past him and pulled his walker out of the snow, then helped him turn. "I don't think it's there, Joey. We should probably report it to Petey, even though he won't be able to return immediately."

He nodded agreement but looked unhappy.

"You two can stay over, and we'll figure out how to get you home tomorrow. There's still food in the kitchen, and I'll bring you some blankets." Freida went upstairs and Marge said, "Why do we keep getting detained in this house?"

<hr />

Gathering in the kitchen, James commiserated with Joey over the potential loss of the UTV and reached into a cupboard for a bottle of whiskey. "Anybody interested in a wee dram?"

Four hands went up, including both of Marge's. "What time is it, anyway?" she asked.

"It's only six, but it feels like midnight. I'm supposed to work tonight, but I think we'll have to close the factory." James handed her a glass. He finished pouring for everyone and then excused himself to notify the milk plant staff of the closure.

Returning after a few minutes, the other three looked up from a Scrabble board. "We found entertainment," Freida smiled at him.

He glanced upstairs and looked disappointed for a moment, but remembered his manners, sitting next to his wife and collecting his tiles.

<hr />

After two glasses of whiskey and two games of Scrabble, Marge wanted to go outside and play in the snow. No one else was interested in that particular pastime, but James agreed to accompany her to the circular drive to investigate the disappearance of the UTV. They weren't gone long.

The snow continued to fall, and icy wind blew from the North. Marge's boots were soon filled with snow, and her hair was frozen. Verifying that the UTV was not where Joey left it, James gawked as Marge fell backward with her arms extended in an attempt to make a snow angel. She landed a foot deep and needed James to pull her out. Then, shivering so violently she could hardly walk, she allowed him to guide her back inside.

Shaking the snow off their coats and boots, Marge told James she might need another warming drink. "A big one."

"I might need one too." He nudged her shoulder with his elbow.

Joey waited silently.

"I'm sorry, Joey. It's not there." She wished it was. He looked distraught. "Did you call Petey?"

"Yes, but you were right, of course. They have a lot of emergencies tonight, and he won't be able to get out here until tomorrow or the next day."

"At least you notified him so they will have the theft on file. Perhaps the police will apprehend the thief touring around on it tonight. It's better that we're indoors."

Joey looked surprised. "What have you done with Marge? She never wants to be indoors when it's snowing."

Marge shivered. "It is absolutely glacial out there. I attempted to fashion a snow angel, and if James hadn't been present, you would have found me frozen in a block of ice tomorrow morning."

Handing her a generous glass of whiskey, James chuckled. "We would have gone looking for you."

She took a sip of whiskey and shuddered. "Either I'm getting old, or this is the coldest weather we've had in a very long time."

As she sat in front of the fire, wrapped in a blanket, sipping her drink, Marge's eyes began to close.

Chapter 25

Freida took Marge's glass as she nodded off, and Joey added a log to the fire and turned off the lights. "Will you be okay down here?" Freida asked.

"I'll just grab a blanket and bunk down on the sofa."

"Do you need a space heater?"

"I don't think so. I'm a light sleeper so I can just add wood if the fire starts to die down."

"There's one in the kitchen if you change your mind."

"Thank you. I'm sorry to cause you so much trouble."

"You're no trouble at all," James said. "Just let us know if you need anything." He took Freida's hand. "Let's get some rest. Who knows what tomorrow will bring."

The two of them said goodnight and closed the door behind them. Joey put an extra blanket on Marge and smiled as she snuggled into the large recliner. Adding more wood to the fire, he took two blankets to the sofa, made himself as comfortable as possible and closed his eyes. When he opened them again, three hours later, Marge's face was two inches from his own. Kneeling in front of the sofa where he lay, she was urgently whispering his name.

Joey worked on regulating his breathing. "Marge, you startled me. What is it? What's the matter?"

"I must use the ladies' room and there's someone moving around out there. Maybe it's James or Freida, but I don't think so. I'm afraid. How would anyone get into the house now?"

Joey scrunched his brow. He could hear a string of anxious stinkers and thought his damaged olfactory sense might be a blessing at the moment. "What time is it?"

"About one."

"We'd better investigate." He pulled on his clothes over his long underwear, stuck his flashlight in his back pocket, and put on his shoes. "Are you warm enough?"

"I'm wearing everything but my winter coat so I should be alright."

Joey grabbed his walker and using the retractable wheels, he inched toward the door to the lavatory. Marge opened it quietly and peeked through the crack. "I don't see anyone," she whispered. "Let me lock the door on the other side."

"I'll stand guard while you're in there and then we can look around."

"Should I refrain from flushing?"

"Probably. You can do that later, after we figure out if we have an intruder."

He waited outside the door and when she rejoined him, they quietly left the sitting room and reconnoitered the perimeter of the first floor.

The doors to each room were closed for heating purposes, making stealth problematic. A strong gust of frigid air hit them when they opened the ballroom door. The French doors to the patio stood wide open, the wind blowing gusts of snow onto the newly refinished floor and causing the temperature of the room to equal that of the outdoors.

Marge immediately advanced toward the open doors, but Joey stopped her. "This would be an ideal location for an ambush. Wait just a moment."

He closed the inner doors behind them and indicated that Marge follow the wall to the right as he went to the left, where the curtained alcove and the stage were located. Keeping one eye on Marge, he carefully approached the alcove.

Swiftly yanking open the curtain and turning on his flashlight, he witnessed the door on the other side of the small space pull shut. Rather than pursue the intruder, he called James and crossed the ballroom to inspect the French doors.

"Hello," James answered groggily.

"We have an intruder," Joey whispered into the phone. "He seems to have gained entrance through the ballroom doors. They were standing wide open when we arrived. Last I saw of him was the door to the alcove shutting behind him. He's somewhere on the first floor. Marge is with me in the ballroom."

"On my way."

Joey disconnected and continued his inspection. "I think this was a decoy," he whispered to Marge. "There aren't any footprints outside, and the lock isn't broken." He returned his phone to his pocket before locking the doors.

Marge had taken up a broom and attempted to brush some of the snow outside beforehand, then she laid some rags on the damp floor to minimize the damage. "Then how did he gain entrance? And why didn't the alarm sound?"

"I don't know. There must be another entrance we don't know about. We should find out if a deputy is still on duty in the basement. If he is, he must be very cold and possibly hungry. If not, the intruder could have broken down the door to the passages."

Marge quietly followed him into the alcove, which led into the sitting room. Exiting into the foyer, they met with James, who was turning on the lights.

"There's no need for stealth. He knows we know he's here, but he could have entered the secret passages from here so it will be difficult to find him now."

"Unless he doesn't know about them," Marge said.

"Maybe we should leave the lights out, so he doesn't know where we are. We could split up. Where's Freida?"

"She's in our room with Paws. I didn't think about the secret passages because their exterior entrance has been blocked off. Do you know if he's armed?"

"No, I didn't see him or her. Let's turn out the lights and come up with a plan."

Joey led the way to the area behind the staircase, where they waited a few minutes for their eyes to adjust, and to listen.

"I need to go get Freida," James whispered. "Stay here and listen for movement."

He left them, and they heard his quiet footsteps on the stairs above them.

A soft rustling sound came from the study, and Marge placed her hand on Joey's arm. "I hear it. I wonder what he's doing."

"Looking for something?"

"Let's see if we can sneak up on him."

Tiptoeing across the foyer, Joey handed Marge his flashlight, and she stuck her head around the doorway to the study, training the flashlight on the intruder.

Standing in front of the desk, its drawers wide open, Nicole froze when the powerful beam of light hit her face.

"Nicole? Aren't you supposed to be in the hospital?" Marge flicked the overhead light on. "Are you here by yourself?"

"Yes."

"What are you looking for? Perhaps we can help you locate it."

Nicole stared silently at Marge.

"How did you enter the house?" Joey asked.

James, Freida, and Paws entered the room, and Nicole broke down completely. Her shoulders slumped and she began to cry. "I unscrewed the hinges on the basement door. I'm looking for a small, very old book."

"Would that be the journal written by Abraham Rutherford?"

Nicole nodded.

"I had my nephew lock it up at the police station, but I have copies if you'd like one."

"Why did you have him lock it up?"

Joey thought the incredulous expression on Marge's face was priceless, then she laughed. "Are you hungry, dear?"

They all decided they were hungry, and Joey wanted to check on the door to the secret passages. Marge and Freida began setting out food; James produced a key to the kitchen passage.

The steps that led from the kitchen to the basement were particularly difficult for Joey as they were narrow and without a handrail. James took the walker and preceded him, so Joey could use his back for balance.

First, searching all the rooms downstairs, they restored the hinges, and James pounded some nails into the door jamb to prevent a similar occurrence in the immediate future.

They then went to look at the tunnel entrance and found Deputy Bloom lying unconscious and suffering from hypothermia. James carried him upstairs and into the sitting room before returning to assist Joey.

He relocked the door behind them and studied Nicole. "You said you came here alone."

"I did."

"How did you enter the basement?"

"I entered through the back door. Mr. Rutherford gave me a key."

"So, you knocked the policeman unconscious before you let yourself into the house?"

"No! Of course not. I didn't see a policeman."

"Well, there he is, in the sitting room. Perhaps he can tell us what happened once he's awake. I can tell you this, if we have an unknown person wandering around in the secret passages, I am going to be very upset. Are you sure you have no idea who might have followed you here?"

Nicole's eyes were wide, and her breathing was shallow, but she shook her head.

"Since we don't know if we have another intruder, we will have to stick together until we can get help. I don't think we should leave Dennis alone. Can I just take something with me?"

Handing him a plate, Freida groaned. "I need more sleep. We need to get some cots."

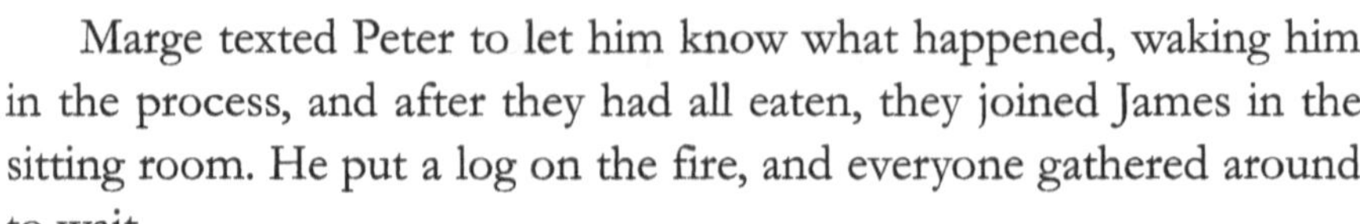

Marge texted Peter to let him know what happened, waking him in the process, and after they had all eaten, they joined James in the sitting room. He put a log on the fire, and everyone gathered around to wait.

When they heard sirens in the distance, Marge bounced up and looked out the window. "It's like a parade!" she declared.

Nicole inched her way toward the door.

"Sit down," James said firmly.

Perching nervously on the edge of the love seat, she watched Joey leave the room.

The snowplow preceded the ambulance and Peter's cruiser. It drove in a nonstop loop to continue clearing roads. Joey opened the door and directed the first responders to the sitting room, where they attended to the deputy.

"I got special authorization because of a fallen officer. What's going on here?" Peter asked.

Joey explained about Nicole and finding Deputy Bloom.

"And someone stole your UTV. Do you have any idea when that happened?"

"No. We didn't realize it was snowing until around five o'clock. Has the plow cleared the way to our street? Or downtown?"

"I don't know. I can radio and ask. Our first order of business was to get the road clear enough to get out here and transport Deputy Bloom to the hospital. Sergeant Dawson will take his place. I'll need to take Ms. Reid to the station for questioning, and possibly for her own safety.

Let me speak with the paramedics, then I'll try to find out about the snowplow." Joey followed him into the sitting room and watched the activity buzz around him for a moment, before sitting next to Marge on the sofa.

"Remember yesterday morning when I said I wanted to come if we weren't entangled for an extended period of time?"

Joey almost laughed. "Have you developed psychic abilities?"

"I certainly hope not."

Peter approached them before he left with Nicole. He motioned James and Freida over and said, "The plow driver has agreed to clear a path to Marge's house before heading back downtown. Joey suggested that it might be safer for you to leave until we've been able to search the passages, and I agree with him. Lock everything up and set the alarm, and we'll get a team out here as soon as we can. Let's shovel a path and make sure one of the cars will start." Peter looked at James. "Is that okay?"

"Freida and I gave up her apartment in town. We don't have anywhere to stay."

Marge linked her arm through Freida's. "You can shelter with Joey or me and bring Paws of course."

"I can bunk at Marge's house if you want your privacy. Can't I?" Joey asked Marge.

"Certainly, although you might want to take a few groceries. Joey usually eats at my house." Marge glanced at Paws, sleeping in front of the fire. "Paws should definitely stay at Joey's because of Fluster."

"Well, let's get a move on then," Peter said. "Keep an eye on the artist," he whispered to Joey, who nodded that he would.

Chapter 26

After leaving Rutherford Mansion, Peter returned to the station with Nicole Reid. It was the middle of the night, but he had decided that their interview couldn't wait. He led Nicole into an interview room and asked if she had any identification, then upon receiving a shake of her head, asked her to wait and left in search of the female deputy on duty.

When they returned to the interview room, Peter sat across from Nicole and said, "Since you have no ID, Officer Carter is going to take your fingerprints then bring you back here for your interview. You are not under arrest, but we need to talk about what's been happening at the Rutherford place and the part you've played. I don't want anyone else to get hurt, and I'm sure you don't either."

Nicole nodded and silently followed Deputy Carter out of the room.

Peter checked in with the officers he had posted at the mansion while he waited, then stood as Carter returned with Nicole. They all took seats around the table and Peter began recording the interview.

"Let's start with Douglas Taft. How did you know him?"

"He owns the gallery where I sell my paintings."

"And he invited you to the housewarming party. Why?"

"He knew I was living there and both of us wanted to see what was going on."

"When the lights went out and Mark Stubbs was stabbed, what happened?"

"I thought Mr. Taft might be in danger, so I took him into the secret passage."

"Why did you think he was in danger?"

"I heard someone threaten him."

"What happened after you entered the passage?"

"I took him to the third floor and told him to wait for me. I wanted to see if it was safe."

"Was it?"

"I don't know, and when I returned to the third floor, Mr. Taft was gone. I looked for him, but finally went back to the basement."

"Do you know where he is now?"

Nicole shook her head.

"But you know he is dead."

Her mouth opened, then it shut. Her eyes were very wide.

"Was he dead when you left him?"

"I didn't hurt him. I swear."

Taking pity on her, Peter said, "He died of a massive heart attack. There was nothing you could have done."

Nicole quivered.

"Why did you leave the hospital yesterday?"

"I wanted to find something I left at the house."

"How did you get there?"

"I took a taxi to the milk plant, then walked."

"About what time was that?"

"I don't know. In the morning?"

Peter made a note. "Easy enough to check since there's only one taxi company in town. Where was the deputy while you were waiting around?"

"I don't know." She shrugged. "I didn't look in the tunnel."

Canting his head to the side and studying her, Peter went on with his next question. "What were you looking for?"

"A small, leather-bound book. It was very old. Your aunt told me she gave it to you for safekeeping but that I could have a copy."

"What's important about that book?"

"I-I'm not sure."

"Someone told you to get the book."

Nicole looked away.

"Was it your husband? Gary Marshall?"

"No." She looked up sharply.

"Do you know his whereabouts?"

"No."

"He hasn't been living with you in the basement?"

"No."

"Someone has been living there with you. Is he violent?"

"He can be."

"Why did he beat you and leave you to die of exposure?"

"He thought I told you about him. He said he was coming back."

"Why do you want to protect him? Do you love him?"

Nicole sealed her mouth shut and studied Peter. Finally, she said, "This is about more than just me."

"What do you mean by that?"

A tear leaked from the corner of her eye, and she trembled. "I have a son, a young boy, who's in long-term hospital care. He told me something bad would happen to my son if I talked."

"What if I post a deputy at the hospital to make sure your son is safe?"

"There are ways he could get to him. Someone dressed as a nurse or delivering meals. It might not matter if there's a guard."

"Well, it can't hurt, so let's start there. We'll take as many precautions as we can. What's your son's name?"

"Alan Marshall. He's in the children's ward."

"We'll send someone immediately." Peter motioned to Deputy Carter to make the call. "Now, let's continue. Why are you living in the basement? Couldn't you sell more paintings and move somewhere more comfortable?"

"At first, he said that we could live there for free and save money, and that no one would know where we were. That appealed to me. But I think he wanted to stay because he was looking for something."

"Like what?"

"I don't know. Something in that book.

There are maps in the book, but he wouldn't let me read it."

"Could you have sold your paintings and left?"

"When the hospital gave me a bill, he sold two or three of my paintings and gave me the exact amount to pay the bill. I don't know how much he sold them for, or if he has money stashed away."

"He made sure you didn't have any money of your own."

Nicole nodded unhappily. "And I need to make sure I have enough money to pay for Alan's care."

"Is he armed?"

"I don't know."

"Is there anything you haven't told me? Anything that might put others at risk?"

Nicole started to shake her head, then said, "He stole the old man's off-road vehicle. He took me to the house and dropped me off by the back door last night and told me to get the book, then he left."

"Do you think he parked by the tunnel and entered that way?"

"He was probably checking up on me."

"Do you think it's likely that he followed you into the secret passages?"

"Yes, he would've wanted to keep an eye on what was going on."

"James sealed the entrance shut and set the alarm when we left. Is there any other entrance that you know of?"

"I don't know of one." She paused. "A couple of times he came out of the passage, and I never saw him go in, so I wondered."

Peter thanked her and turned off the recorder. "We have a break area in the back with some cots. I need to sleep a little bit before my morning shift, and I'd like you to stay here too. Deputy Carter is on duty and can sit with you while you sleep. We'll decide what to do in the morning, and hopefully find your 'friend'. Are you sure you won't tell us his name?"

"No, I can't."

Peter took a deep breath to help dispel his frustration but didn't push her. The officers on duty at the mansion would take him into custody as soon as he tried to exit the premises.

When Carter returned, the three of them proceeded to the break room and got settled. Peter woke once when Carter's radio squawked but fell back asleep when she stepped out of the room to answer the call.

Chapter 27

Once they were finally bundled into the car, with small suitcases, food, and Paws, James drove to Joey's house. Stomping across the street, he, Freida, and Marge trudged up and down the walkway and the porch, to make a flat surface for Joey's walker.

Paws joyfully bounded back and forth with them, trying to eat the snow. Joey, having difficulty staying upright because he was laughing so hard, filmed them kicking snow, jumping up and down, and in Marge's case, crawling on all fours and rolling across the porch.

When the path was deemed walker-worthy, Marge opened her front door to her feline torpedo. Fluster was in such a state about his missing meals, that he completely ignored Paws and meowed long and loud like a siren. Paws, enthralled by the snow, paid him no attention.

Handing James his keys and texting him the alarm code, Joey said goodnight and watched him and Freida through the living room window as they unloaded their small bags and their groceries, letting themselves into his house. He thought a moment, then texted them information about the thermostat, the fireplace, and which room to use, reminding them that Seth sometimes let himself in with his own key. "If he's not there now, however, he probably won't show up until the roads are passable," he wrote.

Joining Marge in the kitchen, Joey let out a sigh of relief. "Are you as tired as I am?"

"Unlikely, but exhausted, nonetheless. Would you rather sleep in the spare bedroom upstairs or down here on the sofa?"

"I'd prefer sleeping down here, if you don't mind."

"I'll get a pillow and some blankets."

Joey watched her go upstairs and hoped that his night terrors wouldn't frighten her. Sayuri had left him when she couldn't deal with his trauma, and he didn't want Marge to know how bad it was. She always accepted him, but everyone has their limits.

Marge returned with the blankets and began arranging them on the sofa. "Make yourself comfortable," she said. "You know where everything is."

She gave him a hug and once again ascended the stairs to her room.

When Marge rose, late that morning, she found Joey in the kitchen, wearing one of her frilly aprons with a cookbook surrounded by measuring cups and spoons, flour, eggs, and milk. She watched him for a moment before asking, "Would you like me to do that?"

Turning abruptly, he squashed an egg in his hand and grimaced. "The instructions looked fairly simple."

"It takes a little practice cooking them. I could help if you'd like to learn how."

"I'd like that." He grinned. "As long as I don't have to make them every time. I happen to love your pancakes."

With Marge's assistance, he quickly had the batter ready. She helped him adjust the burner and showed him how to wait for the bubbles before turning them over. "For some reason, the pan seems to accumulate heat as you cook them, so you have to turn it down as you go, or they end up either burnt or raw in the middle." They made several batches then sat down to eat.

"I wonder how James and Freida are doing."

"I imagine we'll find out presently. They might be sleeping in."

"*We* slept in."

Marge looked at the clock with surprise. "It's almost eleven! How long have you been up?"

"Don't worry. I slept in too." His brow wrinkled. "I wanted to ask you… did I…"

Marge knew what he was worrying about. "I slept like a log, Joey. Nothing short of Fluster biting my toes could have disturbed my sleep, and I locked him out of my room this morning."

Joey's shoulders relaxed and he smiled at her. "Thanks."

"I am not her," she assured him. "Now help me with these dishes."

She turned on the radio and ran hot, soapy water into the sink. Singing and dancing around the kitchen as they worked, they almost missed the knock on the front door. Marge's ears were sharp, though, and she danced her way to the front door. She opened it to find Sergeant Dawson on the stoop, grinning from ear to ear.

Sitting at the curb was Joey's beloved UTV. "Oh, Sergeant, you have just made someone very happy." She turned to call Joey just as he came around the corner from the kitchen and saw his eyes light up.

"You found it!"

James and Freida were crossing the street from his house and saw the UTV sitting there too, and James let out a whoop. "Where was it? Did you catch the thief?"

"No, but we were tipped off about its location."

"I guess the big question is how to keep it from getting stolen again. Whoever took it didn't have a key."

"Oh, here's the key you left with Sergeant Locke." He handed the key to Joey. "Were the doors locked?"

"I don't remember. Maybe not. There were a lot of people at the house when we arrived, and I knew most of them."

"I'd better go. My ride is waiting." Dawson indicated the cruiser idling behind Joey's UTV. "I'm glad I could be the one to return your vehicle. We don't always have such happy endings."

"Thank you, officer." Joey shook his hand and gave him a wave as he left, then turned to James and Freida. "Did you sleep well?"

"We did. Thanks for letting us stay over," James said.

"You might need to stay another day or two. We'll have to check with Peter. I'll give him a call."

"Ask him if they need help with the search."

Joey dialed but got no answer, so he sent Peter a text, asking about their progress."

Ten minutes later, Marge answered the door to find him on the stoop. "Petey! We were just talking about you and surmising your progress."

"That's why I came. Any chance of a cup of coffee?"

"Of course." She linked her arm through his and walked with him into the kitchen, letting go to pour him a cup. Everyone else in the room began talking at once.

"Hold on." He put his hands in the air. "I'll fill you in, but let me get my coat off, will you?" Removing his coat, he sat at the table and accepted his coffee. "Now, where should I start?"

"The last we heard, you were taking Nicole to the station," Joey said.

"Yes, so you locked the doors and set the alarm, and I left two officers and their dogs outside to keep watch, but they didn't detect any movement." He took a sip of coffee. "In our interview with Nicole, we found out that she has a son in the hospital, and the man she has been living with stole Joey's UTV and told her to retrieve the journal. She is married to Gary Marshall, the escaped convict, but says she doesn't know his whereabouts."

"Where is she now?" Marge asked.

"She's still at the station, and we have officers watching her son's room. I don't think either of them is safe until we find the mystery man."

"Have you searched the house already?" James asked.

"No, we'll start in about half an hour, but we're stretched pretty thin, even with officers from Chesterville, and I want everyone to search in pairs; he may be armed. Hugh and his construction crew have volunteered to help. Are you still interested?"

"Yes."

Freida grasped his arm and got a pinched look on her face. "I don't want anything to happen to you."

"I'll be fine. Don't worry."

"You can stay here with us while they search, then when they arrest him, you'll be able to return home." Marge patted her hand. "How is Paws, by the way?"

"He's fine, no matter where he is, as long as someone's feeding him."

"Aunt Marge, I have an assignment for you."

Marge sat up straight and looked at Peter expectantly.

"I need you to read through that journal, paying particular attention to the maps and descriptions of the secret passages. There may be another entrance to the mansion, where our suspect could escape, or might have already. If you find any information, either text or call me."

"Aye, aye, captain." She saluted. "If you have an additional copy, Freida can help."

"I brought two. The three of you can work together to find the information as quickly as possible." He passed a copy to Joey and one to Freida before taking a final gulp of coffee and getting to his feet. "Ready, James?"

James stood and nodded, bending to give Freida a kiss on the cheek, and telling her not to worry, before following Peter out to his cruiser.

Chapter 28

The fire in Marge's living room was crackling merrily as Marge, Joey, and Freida, each with a copy of the journal, sat reading. It was slow work due to the author's painfully cramped, cursive writing, which was legible, but sometimes difficult to decipher. They stopped every thirty minutes or so to discuss what they had read.

Marge found the section detailing the secret passages and, after reading the explanatory text, began studying the maps. When they had reached their second break, she held up a finger and asked for a little more time, so the others continued to read as she studied the maps. When she was finished, she sat quietly for a few minutes, thinking about what she had learned, then she set the papers in her lap and looked at her friends. "I have located the information we seek."

Joey put his copy down and Freida leaned forward.

"I discovered a meticulous map of the passages and an explanation of why they were integrated into the mansion. The author seems to have been extremely paranoid and wanted ways for his guests and himself to enter and exit his home without being seen and to escape, should he find himself under attack. The passages also allowed him to spy on visitors he deemed suspicious.

"The maps in the book are similar to what our first search party documented, but two additional passages exist. I don't know if they've been blocked off, but they don't connect to the main passages and are better concealed. Peruse page sixty-three." She waited for them to find the page in their copies. "Observe these two passages that lead outside; they aren't connected to the others. Petey's suspect could have departed precipitously."

"Where do the passages lead?" Joey stared at the map, searching for landmarks.

"I believe one leads toward the forest, behind the maze, and one leads toward the far side of the property."

"Can you describe the passages to Peter, or do we need to go over there?"

"I believe we should report in person. Will the UTV accommodate the three of us?"

"We might have to squeeze, but none of us are very big."

"Let's go then."

Marge texted Peter on the way, and he was waiting for them when they arrived. Joey pulled right up to the front entrance and made sure the doors to the UTV were locked. Handing Peter a copy of the journal opened to the map, Marge pointed out the two passages. "Even with officers posted outside, you might have missed his departure, but once he exited the passage, he would have to deal with two feet of snow. He might not have gotten far, depending on what time he began."

"He might also be holed up at the end of one of the passages. I'll send two teams of officers to find out. Come with me because you're good at finding the release mechanisms."

Calling the teams on his radio, Peter walked with Marge into the ballroom where she crawled around on the stage and under it. She finally found a trap door, camouflaged to look like a section of boards built to hold stage scenery. Swinging the two by fours that surrounded it outward, she lifted the square piece of flooring with the attached leather strap. Looking inside, she saw metal rungs descending into darkness and she shivered. *No more secret passages for me.*

"This one leads to an area on the far side of the property.

"If you drew a triangle, the base running from the house to the stone hut, the exit would be at the pinnacle. It might be difficult to spot from the outside, but Joey could probably pick you up once you exit," Marge told the officers.

"We don't know if the suspect is armed," Peter said. "Sending Joey could put him in danger." He turned to his men. "Radio with a report when you reach the end of the passage."

"Yes, sir." The two men descended the ladder one at a time.

Peter consulted the map. "Where is the other one?"

"It looks like it might start behind the fireplace in the dining room." Marge headed out of the ballroom, Peter jogging to catch up with her. She poked around, finally finding the catch that opened a narrow entrance. "I guess he must have been a small man. James would not be able to pass through."

Joey, who had been trailing in their wake, snickered at Marge's observation.

Peter radioed his second team.

"Where's Freida?" Marge asked.

"She was in the foyer when we passed through."

"Let's locate her. She shouldn't be wandering around alone." They were about to leave the dining room when Peter's second team of officers arrived with Freida.

"Where have you been?" Marge asked.

"I was just looking in each room to see if anything has been rearranged or taken, but I didn't find any evidence that anyone was ever here."

"Maybe he left soon after we did," Peter said. "We have no way of knowing." He gave team two the same instructions he gave the first team and told Marge, Joey, and Freida that they were free to return home.

"Where's James?"

"He's in the passages with Hugh and Dawson. Do you want him to call you when he gets back?"

"Yes, please."

Marge didn't want to miss out on the action, but he assured her she would receive an update, so she grudgingly acquiesced.

"Let's go to the Fireside for lunch," Joey suggested. "We can bring something back for James."

Squishing into the UTV once again, Joey drove them downtown and parked at the curb, only to find the restaurant temporarily closed. Marge groaned in disappointment. "Let's drive by The Dark Horse before we go home, to see if it's closed too."

"Isn't that the dive motorcycle bar?" Freida asked.

"Yes. Have you ever been there?"

Freida glanced at Marge. "No. James won't let me."

Marge's eyebrows rose.

Joey drove toward the bar and found the parking lot empty except for one black pickup truck. He stopped the UTV and said, "Those tires must be almost as tall as Freida."

"Hey. I resemble that remark."

"Should we see if it's open?"

"We'll have to park right by the door, and I'll need some help getting through the snow."

"Park and I will determine if it's open before you go through the trouble of getting up the steps."

Joey nodded and pulled up right next to the steps. Marge disembarked, then plowed through the snow, filling her boots in the process. The door opened when she pushed on the handle and she peeked through the opening, her eyes trying to adjust to the dim light.

An enormous, bald man, wearing jeans and a flannel shirt, stood behind the bar drying glasses. "Can I help you?" His voice was surprisingly deep and seemed to echo through the establishment.

"My friends and I were passing and wondered if you were open."

"I am. Come on in."

"Do you serve food, by any chance?"

"Yes, but since I'm the only one here today it will have to be something very simple."

"Simple is fine." Marge smiled. "We'll be right in."

Marge returned to the UTV and said, "They're open, and they have simple food. Come on." She and Freida helped Joey inside and they sat at a table near the bar.

The bartender brought them menus and paused when his eyes met Joey's, but Joey gave no sign of recognition, so the man backed away saying, "Remember, something simple. I'm not a very skilled cook."

"Could we get drinks while we decide?" Marge asked.

"Sure. What can I get you."

"I'd like a whiskey, neat."

"Me too. How about you, Freida?"

"Could you add some Coke to mine?" she asked meekly.

"No problem. I'll be back in a minute to take your order."

Joey watched him walk away but didn't say anything immediately.

"Do you think he might poison us?" Marge whispered.

"No, I think he's hoping I don't recognize him. Later, okay? Decide what you want to eat."

"Quesadillas are easy, right?"

"I don't cook at all, so I'm not the right person to ask."

"You know how to make pancakes now."

"True. I'm okay with a quesadilla. How about you?" He looked at Freida.

"Sure, and maybe some chips or fries. I'm pretty hungry. And we have to get something for James."

The bartender returned with their drinks, setting them carefully on the table. "Have you decided?"

"Are quesadillas simple?" Marge asked.

"Yeah." He smiled faintly.

"What about fries?" Freida asked.

"Sure. The individual pizzas are frozen so I can make those too."

"Ooh. Pizza. That sounds good too. Why don't we get three quesadillas, two pizzas, and an order of fries?"

Joey shrugged. "Okay by me."

"And something for James. Could we get a quesadilla to go?"

"Do you want me to make it when you're about done so it won't get cold?"

"Yes, thank you. It will probably be cold by the time I get it home anyway, but at least it will have a fighting chance."

They all chuckled, and Marge noticed that the man had loosened up somewhat and didn't appear as nervous as he did when they first entered.

As they sat and waited for their food, someone entered the kitchen from the back door and appeared to be arguing with the bartender. Marge couldn't see him very well through the opening, but he looked about the same size. She surreptitiously took out her phone and snapped a couple of pictures.

"What are you doing? They might see you," Joey said.

"I'm busy," they heard the bartender say. "Just go upstairs and wait."

The visitor rounded the corner from the kitchen and went through a door they hadn't noticed before. He turned as he opened the door, and Joey said something to Marge so he wouldn't see the surprise on her face.

"What is it?" Freida asked, but the bartender was headed for their table with a tray of food, so Marge and Joey started talking about their visit to the tree farm.

"Here you are folks. Can I get you another drink?"

"Sure," Marge answered for all of them. "Everything looks delicious."

He left again, returning with fresh drinks, and said, "Enjoy," before heading back behind the bar.

"Let's talk about the Christmas party now," Marge suggested. "Do you think this mess will be cleared up in time?"

"Hopefully. Should we make it a dinner party?" Freida took a big bite of pizza. "This is surprisingly good for frozen."

"That might be the whiskey talking," Joey said with a grin. "Although, I am also finding it quite tasty."

"I prefer the quesadilla. I wonder what kind of cheese they use. I use cheddar at home, but this has a different taste." She froze when the bartender, who had approached when she wasn't looking, said, "It's pepperjack."

Marge gaped at him. "You startled me."

"Sorry. I wondered if you wanted me to get started on your to-go order."

"Yes, thanks for remembering. We got so caught up in eating that I think we all forgot," Joey said.

"James' stomach would never forgive me." Freida giggled.

"Ok, that's it. No more whiskey for you, young lady." Marge pretended to swipe her drink.

"Hey."

Marge laughed and returned her drink as the bartender turned around and reentered the kitchen.

Turning serious, Marge said, "When we were reading the journal, did either of you read anything about a treasure?"

"Toward the end, when he was sick, Abraham alluded to secreting valuables for future generations of Rutherfords. He wrote that the key could be found in the pages of the journal," Joey said.

"Did you find the key?"

He shook his head.

"Nothing about treasure?"

Freida looked at Marge. "I read something about treasure. It was a quote. Hold on a second." She pulled out her copy of the book and flipped through it, before handing it to Marge. "Right there." She pointed.

"*The hidden well-spring of your soul must needs rise and run murmuring to the sea,*" Marge read. "*And the treasure of your infinite depths would be revealed to your eyes.*"

"I looked it up," Freida said. "It's a quote from Kahlil Gibran's 'The Prophet'."

"Interesting," Joey murmured. "But that doesn't seem to be the same type of treasure, does it?"

The bartender returned as they finished their meal and asked if they were ready to pay their bill. Joey paid with cash and told him to keep the change.

Exiting the building, they discovered that the temperature had dropped, and the snow had frozen solid, making the short trip back to the UTV treacherous.

They all managed to climb inside, and Marge pointed out the sign in the window had changed to 'closed' as they sat warming up the engine.

They were in clear view of the black pickup truck when the bartender and his visitor left through the back exit and got in, but the two men either didn't see them or ignored them, clanking on giant, chain-covered tires as they roared out of the parking lot.

"That bartender is the man who tried to assault me in the maze," Joey said.

Marge gaped at him. "No wonder he looked alarmed. Did you see who his visitor was?"

"Yes. The caretaker."

"I can't believe we sat there and ate and drank what he served us," Freida said. "He could have poisoned all of us."

"It was very important to convince him I didn't recognize him."

"They look very alike, don't they? Did you text Petey?"

"I did. I was thinking we'd follow them, but the frozen snow doesn't leave nice tracks like the powder did."

"It's better we don't put Freida in danger anyway. James would have our heads."

"I'm right here," Freida complained.

"I know, dear." Marge patted her hand.

Chapter 29

Peter stared at Joey's text in dismay. He ran his broad, freckled hand through his auburn hair, something he seemed to be doing a lot. Then he re-read the text.

"Caretaker and maze assailant left Dark Horse together in black Tacoma. Unable to follow in UTV."

Why, oh why, can't they stay out of it? Peter had to admit the information was helpful, but those two drove him crazy. *What do I do now? I don't know where they're headed and even if I did, I don't have anyone to send.* His officers were spread thin.

Determining that the mansion was their most likely destination, Peter left the station and headed in that direction. His radio crackled to life as he drove.

"Officer down," came a weak voice. "Officer and one civilian down at the old stone hut on the Rutherford property."

Peter's heart began to race, and he pressed his foot more firmly on the accelerator.

Dawson was breathing shallowly, his voice becoming fainter. "Shooter… dropped weapon… fled… black Toyota Tacoma. Request assistance."

The radio went dead. "Dawson?" Peter shouted into his radio. "Dawson!" Receiving no response, he called for medical assistance and radioed Holmes and Carter. "Report to the old stone hut immediately. I'll meet you there."

Sweating profusely, his cruiser bouncing across the uneven ground between the mansion and the hut, Peter wasn't thinking clearly. He had forgotten to put out an APB on the Tacoma and alert the chief. He skidded to a stop in the clearing and ran toward Sergeant Holmes' all-terrain vehicle. The powerful searchlight mounted on the roof was pointed toward the stone hut.

Holmes and Surge were scanning the area, and Carter was on the radio.

"Yes, sir," she said and clipped her radio to her belt.

Peter at once realized his mistake. "Was that the chief?"

Carter nodded.

"Have you found Dawson?"

Carter pointed toward Surge, who whined and sat next to Holmes.

"Carter!" Holmes shouted.

Peter and Carter approached to find Holmes on her knees, checking for a pulse. Shaking her head, she rose and took out her phone. Peter stood frozen as she began to take preliminary photos.

"Where is the civilian victim?"

"This way," Carter said. "He's still alive."

Peter knelt by the victim and studied his face, then turned when he heard the sirens.

Chief Lloyd approached him as the paramedics were loading Dawson into the ambulance. He stood with his feet frozen in place and stared vacantly as his friend and co-worker was whisked away.

Placing a hand on Peter's shoulder, the chief said, "Locke?"

Peter didn't respond. He was not new to the job. He had seen plenty of death. But Peter had never lost a brother and he blamed himself. He was filled with grief and guilt.

"Locke, are you okay?"

Peter nodded vacantly.

"Someone needs to notify his family."

"I'll go, Chief." He forced himself to walk. Returning to his cruiser, he slowly drove to Sergeant Dawson's house with no idea of what to say to his wife.

Pulling up to the curb in front of the house, Peter remained in his cruiser, but no words came to him. He walked reluctantly to the front door and knocked. When Fred's wife answered, she automatically smiled at Peter until she saw the look on his face.

"No," she cried. "Tell me it's not Fred." She grabbed the front of Peter's shirt. "Tell me he's okay."

Peter's mouth crumpled and a tear rolled down his cheek. "I'm so sorry."

"Nooo," she keened. "Where is he?"

"He's at the morgue," Peter whispered. "I'm so sorry."

Fred's little girl, a child of four, peeked around her mother's leg and said, "What's wrong, mommy?"

Carrie picked up the little girl and hugged her as she cried, and Peter fell to his knees and sobbed. Putting the little girl down, she said, "Why don't you go pick out a book to read, and I'll be there in a minute."

"Ok," she said doubtfully.

Once she had gone inside the house, Carrie got down on her knees in front of Peter and hugged him. "What happened?" She shuddered and her shoulders shook.

"I'm not sure what happened, but he was shot. We'll find out."

"How will I explain to Hailey that her daddy's gone and won't be coming back? How will I live without him?"

Peter felt like his soul was being ripped apart. He shakily stood and helped Carrie to her feet, then looked at her misery and hugged her once more. "I would take his place if I could."

"I believe you would," she said, "but it won't bring him back. Thank you for telling me in person, Peter. I need to go talk to Hailey now." She took a deep, shaky breath.

"Let me know if there's anything I can do." He turned away as she closed the door, his heart aching and his words sounding trite and inept to his own ears.

Not much of a drinker, Peter stopped at the liquor store and bought six bottles of hard alcohol before driving home.

He sent a text to Chief Lloyd, asking for a leave of absence, then he turned off his phone and closed his curtains.

Sitting on his sofa with a glass and the bottles, he opened one and took a sip, shuddering at the harshness of the alcohol. He was alone with his thoughts and although he drank steadily, he couldn't drown them out. Drinking until he felt the world tilt and spin, he fell asleep and dreamt of a small child crying for her father.

He woke and began the cycle again.

As a coping mechanism, it wasn't working well, but he didn't know any other way to quiet his thoughts. The phone woke him, so he tore the plug out of the wall socket. Someone banged at his door, so he put on his earphones and turned up the music. He didn't want to see anyone. *No one could possibly understand.* He poured himself another drink.

Hours turned into days as his thoughts turned blacker.

I might as well have killed him myself. I don't deserve to live.

He threw up and fell asleep on the bathroom floor.

Chapter 30

Although Marge rarely watched television, she and Joey watched 'White Christmas' together every year. After yoga and breakfast, they sat in front of the fire and enjoyed the music and pageantry of the on-screen rehearsals. Marge loved the costumes, and they both became misty-eyed at the love the men showed for their former colonel.

An unfamiliar knock on the door roused Marge from her recliner. She paused the movie and glanced at Joey, who raised a brow. Crossing the room to answer the knock, she was surprised to find the Chief of Police standing on her porch. The snow had begun to melt and sat in slushy mountains along the street.

"May I come in?" he asked.

Marge backed up and, remembering her manners, asked if he would like a cup of coffee.

"No, thank you." He twisted his cap in his hands, his white hair standing in a tuft on his bare head. "I know that we haven't always been on the best of terms, but I need your help. I am genuinely alarmed by Peter's reaction to Sergeant Dawson's death. He seems to feel responsible and he's not handling it well. I think he needs someone to talk to."

"Is it affecting his work?" Joey asked.

"He's taken a leave of absence, in the middle of a case," Chief Lloyd said with significance. "Most officers wouldn't do that, and the Peter I know would never do that. He'd want to catch his man, especially if he had shot another officer." He handed Marge a file. "This is confidential, but it might contain information that will help Peter. I'm entrusting it to you for his sake. He's a good officer, and I don't want him to throw his career away without fully understanding what went down."

Marge silently accepted the file, understanding that the chief was going out on a limb for Peter. "Thank you," she said quietly. "We'll take care of it." Marge knew she sounded more certain than she felt, but she could see that she had helped relieve some of his burden and she shook his hand before he left. "Thank you for letting us know."

Once he left, Marge turned to Joey and said, "This is more your line of expertise than mine. Do you think you can help him?"

"Perhaps. We'll have to see how bad it is."

Marge nodded. "Can we go now?"

"Yes. We should take him something to eat. Do we have any leftover sandwiches?"

"You read the file while I prepare something."

Peter's curtains were drawn, and he didn't answer Marge's knock, but she persisted. "Petey, I need to talk to you. Please answer the door. Joey is here with me. Open up." She continued to knock and call to him until he finally opened the door.

His hair was dirty and disheveled, and his eyes were bleary. He was in his boxers and smelled of alcohol. Marge looked around at Peter's domestic chaos and let Joey take the lead.

"Hello, Peter. I hear you're having a rough time," Joey began. "Why don't we sit down and talk about it?" He sat down, and Marge placed the tray of sandwiches on the coffee table.

"What do you know about anything, old man?" Peter slurred.

From the look on her face, Joey suspected Marge was about to whack Peter about the head, so he motioned for her to cease and desist.

"I'll tell you one thing I know. If you don't catch the man who killed Sergeant Dawson, his death will be meaningless. You are an excellent policeman, and you can make sure his killer goes to prison for the rest of his life."

He paused to make sure Peter was listening, then continued. "If you lost your life while performing your duty, wouldn't you want those left behind to make sure the perpetrator was put behind bars?"

Peter ran his hand through his hair and took a sandwich square. Then he set it back down as the tears came; violent, heart-wrenching sobs shook him as he gulped for air. At first, he couldn't speak, and then little by little he let it out: the guilt, the shame, the helplessness, the despair, the look on the young widow's face. He drew in a shaky breath." I've never lost a brother. I don't know how you made it through the war, Joey." He began to cry again.

"Death is hard in any situation, but people in law enforcement and the military, we've gone through the trenches together and have sworn to have each other's backs. We have a special bond and feel responsibility for each other's safety. You work in a dangerous profession, where death is a possibility on any given day, but the irony, perhaps, is that bond, that feeling of responsibility, makes death even harder to cope with."

"It was my fault." Peter's shoulders shook, and his hands clenched. "I posted him there by himself. He should have had backup."

"Did you know two men were going to show up? Did you know one of them would have a gun? Did you tell him to stay hidden and record them? Could you have predicted that he would trip and draw fire? Do you really think that with backup he would have done something different?"

Peter's breath became slightly more even, and he picked up his sandwich again. "I guess not." He took a bite. "He was that kind of dedicated officer. He wanted evidence, and he would have tried to get it even if he had a partner with him."

Joey leaned forward. "Sergeant Dawson was a good officer, just like you, and he would have suffered like you if anyone else on his team had died.

"You're grieving his loss, and that's very understandable, but what you must do now is get back out there and catch his killer."

Peter thought about that for a few minutes while he ate. "You're right, Joey. I've been selfishly wallowing while Dawson's killer is roaming around a free man." Still drunk, Peter was being somewhat expansive and flinging his arms around, but Joey could see the change in his attitude and the determination in his eyes; he knew Peter would be alright.

Standing, he gestured to Marge. "We'll go now, Peter. Eat those sandwiches, drink lots of water, and get some sleep. Tomorrow morning, I'll expect you at Marge's house for breakfast. We have some information to share." Joey looked back as they let themselves out of Peter's apartment and saw him pick up another sandwich.

"Do you think he'll be okay?" Marge asked, brow furrowed, as they got back into the UTV. "I've never seen him like that."

"I think he'll be fine. He had a big shock and no one to talk to."

"He could have talked to us."

Joey shook his head. "I've been there before. You feel like no one could possibly understand. I was very broken when I returned from the war."

"You didn't turn to drink."

"No, but I still have nightmares."

Marge nodded. She knew that, but Joey didn't talk about it much. "Did you ever feel responsible, like Petey does?"

"There was always that thought in the back of my head. If only I had done this or that, he might still be alive. I think it's part of the grieving process, blaming yourself, blaming others, blaming God."

Marge stared at nothing. "Delivering the news to Dawson's widow must have been especially difficult."

"And his young daughter. Feeling additional guilt for their grief."

"Look," Joey said as they approached his house. "Someone has shoveled my walkway. I'd like to get a change of clothes; mine are getting to the point where they can stand up on their own. Besides, James may have news."

Marge nodded and set her bun bobbing. She and Joey carefully made their way to his front door and knocked, out of politeness.

"You're just in time," James said as he opened the door. "Freida's making ravioli for lunch."

Walking through to the kitchen, Joey asked if they had heard any news about the mansion.

"Hugh called and said the construction crew is sealing up the exit passages from the inside. We'll have to figure out what we want to do long term but for now, making the house secure is a priority."

"I'm almost certain that one of the two men at the stone hut was our intruder, so he can't be in the house."

"Right. Sealing up the passages now, will make sure we don't have to worry about anyone else gaining entrance."

"Have you been comfortable here?"

"Yes. Thank you again for letting us stay. We should be able to return home once we get the car dug out and the chains on."

"Another day or two won't hurt, plus I'm sure you're warmer here. How is Paws faring?"

Freida turned from the stove with a smile. Paws was sitting at her feet, alert, tail thumping at the sound of his name. "Paws is a very spoiled puppy. Aren't you, boy?" His tail thumped faster, but his gaze didn't waver from the stove.

"He is certainly focused." Marge sat at the kitchen table.

"Would you like some coffee? I have some made."

"Thank you, Freida. I could use something warm to take the chill off."

Freida gave the pot another stir and turned the burner down before pouring two mugs of coffee and setting them on the table. "This one's for you, Joey." Pouring two more, she said, "James?"

"I'm almost coffee-ed out but I think I can use one more."

He and Freida joined them at the table.

"Freida's been having second thoughts about the Rutherford place."

"That's reasonable," Marge said. "So much intrigue."

Freida stared into her cup, and Paws walked over to her, laying his head in her lap. Petting him absentmindedly she said, "Every time I went to bed, I woke up to a crisis of some sort. There've been strangers wandering around the house, and we keep finding entrances we didn't know about. I don't feel safe there. The house is so big and with all those secret passages, you never know if someone could pop into your room uninvited. Even if we lock the door, they could come in through the closet." She shuddered.

"She's been having nightmares."

"It might take a while to get past that," Joey said, "but once all of the exits have been sealed, and the intruders detained, it should start to feel safe." He thought for a moment. "It might help when all the rooms are finished as well. Those dark, dilapidated rooms can seem spooky."

"Have we made a mistake?"

"Why don't you just stay here for now, until the investigation is complete? Perhaps Marge and I can help you clean up the rooms on the second floor so they look less like the set of a horror flick."

Freida gave a tentative smile. "That might help, and staying here helps too. A good night's sleep does wonders."

"I'll put a lock on the closet entrance too, so we know we'll be safe in our bed." James laid his hand on hers.

Chapter 31

Marge wasn't too sure how she felt about Joey staying at her house for more than a few days. It shouldn't matter, because they spent all their waking hours together anyway, but somehow it did. *I wonder if Joey feels the same way, like we've temporarily lost our sliver of personal space.* She dressed in her neon pink polyester pantsuit, in an attempt to elevate her mood, and she looked in the bathroom mirror. "Today, I choose happiness," she told her reflection. "Today is a wonderful day." She smiled at herself in the mirror and skipped downstairs.

Joey was sitting at the kitchen table with his chin resting on his hands. Walking up behind him, Marge placed her hands on his shoulders. "You're feeling it too, aren't you?"

He looked up at her unhappily. "I love you, Marge, and I love spending time with you, but I miss sleeping in my own bed."

Rubbing his shoulders, she said, "I know. I was pondering that upstairs. Millicent offered them the use of her house, but I wanted to hear your thoughts before I suggested it."

Joey's eyes lit up. "That sounds like a perfect solution. They wouldn't have to worry about imposing and we could have our... go back to normal. But what if it snows more and we can't get back and forth?"

Marge laughed. "We'll manage somehow. What would you like for breakfast?"

"Let's be wild and have French toast."

"And sausage?"

"Woo! Wild *and* crazy."

They laughed together and drank their coffee before Marge started the sausages.

183

Joey went to answer a knock at the door as she was dishing out their breakfast and returned with Peter.

"You're looking much better today," Marge said.

"I feel much better, thanks to you two."

"Have some breakfast and we'll talk about the latest developments." She handed him a plate and set one down in front of Joey, before dishing out her own. Peter finished first, so Joey handed him the file Chief Lloyd had left with Marge.

"Take a look at this while we finish eating and let me know what you think."

Peter read in silence, then said, "This is how you knew what happened at the stone hut. Where did you get it?"

"Believe it or not, Chief Lloyd gave it to Marge."

Peter gaped at him. "The chief would *never*," he spluttered. "*The chief?*"

"That's how concerned he was."

Peter stared at the file. "I'm sorry I caused so much worry. I had no idea how much my actions would affect everyone. The chief... I didn't know he would even give it a thought."

"He came here in person."

Peter shook his head. "I'm shocked. Truly."

"About what you read in the file. The fingerprints. What do you make of that?"

"The man who was shot is Gary Marshall, Nicole's husband.

Joey nodded. "Does she know?"

"I don't know. The fingerprints on the gun belong to Gary's brother Lawrence. You saw Gary and the caretaker get into the truck, right? It looks like Gary has been hiding in plain sight. He's the man you saw in the pub, the one who tried to assault you in the maze."

"So, what do you think that means?"

"It's difficult to know who did what, but I imagine Lawrence has been posing as the caretaker and keeping his eye on Nicole."

"I'd like to speak to her," Marge said.

"Why would it be more beneficial for you to talk to her, rather than me?"

"Because I'm a woman and not a police officer."

"As far as I know, she's still staying at the station, so you can ride in with me if you like. I can't guarantee Lloyd will remain friendly though." He gave her a wry smile.

Peter's arrival at the station was met with cheers and pats on the back. The chief called him into his office, so he asked the deputy in reception to show Marge into the breakroom to speak with Nicole, before entering the office and closing the door.

Sitting across from Chief Lloyd, Peter saw Marge enter the break room. Lloyd saw her too, and grimaced. "I suppose I'm stuck with her now, aren't I?"

"Not necessarily." Peter gave him a weak smile. "The case is almost closed, and she doesn't really have anything else to investigate, does she?"

"I guess not. Where are we at?"

"Well, Gary Marshall is in intensive care with an officer posted outside his room. We've moved his son into his room so they can be together and to minimize the number of personnel needed."

"Do you think they're still in danger?"

"Yes, until we locate Lawrence."

"Any idea where he might be hiding out?"

"No. We have all the entrances to the mansion sealed off, and officers posted at the mansion, the stone hut, and the pub."

"Perhaps Gary can provide some suggestions. Has his wife been to visit him yet?"

"No."

"Why don't you take her over there after you take your aunt home?"

Peter chuckled. "Yes, sir." He stood to leave and was surprised when the chief stood as well, holding out his hand.

"I'm glad you're back, Locke," he said gruffly.

"Thank you, sir." Peter shook his hand and left the office.

When Marge entered the breakroom, Nicole was sitting at a small round table with a paper cup of coffee, watching television. The deputy left them and closed the door. "Hello, Nicole. I don't know if you remember me?"

Nicole turned. "How could I forget that bun?"

Marge patted her head. "I suppose you have a point. Would you be willing to answer a few questions for me?"

"Why? Do you work for the police?"

"No, but I'm privy to some information they've uncovered, and I wonder if you could help me understand it."

"What does it have to do with you?"

"It really has to do with you and your safety I think."

"Fine. What do you want to know?"

Marge pulled out a chair and sat down. "Do you still love your husband?"

Nicole looked everywhere except at Marge before finally slumping in her chair. "Yes."

"Does he frighten you?"

"No." She sighed. "He went to prison for something his brother did, then when he escaped, they decided to trade places. He has never been a criminal."

"Are you aware that he has been shot?"

Nicole sat up straight and leaned forward. "No! Is he okay?"

"The fingerprints on the gun belong to his brother, Lawrence. Is he the man who's been living with you?"

Putting her head in her hands, Nicole groaned.

"Yes. Will Gary be okay? Can I see him?"

"We can ask. Do you have any idea where Lawrence might be hiding? He shot and killed a police officer as well."

Nicole silently shook her head.

"The authorities know his identity now, and they know he shot his brother and the policeman. They have proof. What they don't know is who stabbed Mark Stubbs and killed Mr. Taft. What was the plan? Were they working together? And why would Lawrence shoot Gary?"

"I just don't know. I think Larry might have killed Mr. Taft because he was getting too friendly with me, but since he was our buyer… It couldn't have been Gary. I'm sure he didn't have anything to do with killing anyone."

Mulling that over, Marge said, "Did you ever meet with Gary?"

"No, he told me to stay away." She attempted to twist her wedding ring, which was no longer on her finger, then folded her hands in her lap. "Larry has a mean streak, and Gary is always having to clean up his messes, and he got worse when the construction crew came, and your friends moved in. But when Larry beat me up and left me in the stone hut, Gary probably went ballistic."

"So, when he tried to assault Joey, he was probably in the middle of cleaning up one of Larry's messes? Sayuri?"

Nicole's eyes went wide. "I don't know everything that went on between them, but I suppose that could be why."

<hr>

Marge and Joey were sitting in the lobby when Peter finished his meeting with the chief. "There you are. Nicole asked if she could see her husband."

"Yes, I'll take her to the hospital as soon as I drive you home. Chief's orders."

"Can't we come too?"

"I don't see why there would be any need for that. I'll let you know how it goes."

"It's okay, Marge. We have to talk to James and Freida anyway." Joey elbowed her.

Marge sighed but went along with Joey's suggestion. They waited for Peter to fetch Nicole, then accepted the ride home.

Chapter 32

Expecting Fluster to bombard her, Marge braced herself when she opened her front door, then looked around in confusion. "Where is he? It's lunch time."

"Maybe he didn't expect you so soon. He's probably taking a nap."

"Why don't you call James and invite him and Freida over for lunch? I'll endeavor to locate my missing feline."

Marge walked around the downstairs, calling, then headed upstairs. The door to her bedroom was open and she took a deep breath before entering. Standing in the doorway, she scanned the room. Fergus' cage was lying on its side, open, and Fluster was in the middle of the bed, tail thumping against the comforter. "Where is he?"

Fluster gazed at her defiantly.

"Did you hurt him?"

Marge sat on the edge of her bed and saw the little lump under the covers when Fluster rose to rub against her arm. It wasn't moving. Filled with dread, Marge gave Fluster a pet and carried him out of the room, closing the door once he was outside.

She walked to the bed and pulled the comforter back, and there was Fergus. Although relieved, Marge's heart wrenched at seeing the tiny mouse clearly terrified, but still breathing. Poor little thing. She picked him up gently and held him against her chest until he knew he was safe, then placed him back in his cage and gave him some fresh food. *I must find a different type of cage. One of these days he won't be so lucky.*

Slowly descending the stairs, she answered a knock on the front door and found Freida and James waiting on the porch.

189

"The snow is starting to melt," Freida said.

"Just enough to make it slushy before it freezes tonight." Joey stood in the entrance to the kitchen and grimaced. "It's sure making it hard for me to get around."

"Shouldn't be too much longer." James smiled. "What's for lunch?"

"I'm not sure yet. I just had a cat and mouse crisis. Any requests?"

Joey glanced at Marge with a raised eyebrow, silently asking if everything was okay.

She gave him a quick nod and a weak smile, with her hand on her heart. "I have some tortillas and cheese. We could have quesadillas again."

"That sounds perfect. I could cut up some green onions and whatever else you'd like to add." Freida hung their coats in the hall closet.

They all strode into the kitchen. "By the way, Millicent offered you the use of her house down the street since she's staying at the Beaumonde house. That way you can remain as long as you like, and Joey will be able to move back into his house."

"That sounds perfect," Freida exclaimed. "Is she okay with Paws staying there?"

"I don't think she'll mind. We'll just have to make sure we vacuum well before she returns."

"I'm excited. She told me she has a jacuzzi."

"You can just leave your car where it is for now," Joey said. "When it thaws, we can put some chains on it."

"We might need to replenish our food supply. Freida eats so much."

Freida looked at James in mock horror, then they both laughed.

"I'll let Millicent know, and maybe we can go to the Fireside for dinner, if it's open."

Marge sent a quick text before she began pulling ingredients from the refrigerator and setting to work shredding cheese.

"I'll call and find out." James pulled out his phone.

"Hi, Curtis. James. I was wondering if you'll be open this evening… Great! See you later then… Okay, bye." He disconnected and grinned at the others. "We're in business. They're open."

"Woo-hoo." Joey threw his arms in the air. "We'll be feasting tonight!"

"These will be ready momentarily. Why don't you start a pot of coffee, you rascal."

Joey got up and winked at Marge. "Yes, ma'am. Such a slave driver." Then he looked toward the kitchen entrance and said, "James, could you get that? Someone's at the door."

James went into the living room and returned a moment later. "That was Millicent's driver. He brought us her key. We'll be able to move over there after lunch. I know it's been inconvenient having us stay, Joey, but I really appreciate it."

"It's probably been better not having to go back and forth in the snow, but I do miss sleeping in my own bed."

Placing the first two quesadillas on plates and using the pizza cutter to make wedges, Marge added two more to the pans on the stove and handed the plates to Freida. "You can each take a piece while I finish cooking these. Does anyone want some sour cream or Tapatio? I like to mix them."

"I'll get them." Freida went to the refrigerator.

Once they were all settled at the table, they made plans to meet at the Fireside at six. "James and I can walk on the plowed roads and you two can take the UTV."

"I would suggest we walk too, but Joey might get mired in the piles of plowed snow."

"It's best to play it safe right now." Freida took their plates to the sink.

"Do you need help carrying things to Millicent's house?"

"We don't have much, and James can always make another trip if he needs to."

"Hrmf. Is that all I am to you, a beast of burden?"

"Of course, dear. You knew that when you married me." She grinned. "Let's go. I can't wait to see our new temporary home."

Marge and Joey saw them off, then returned to the kitchen to clean up the dishes. "What shall we do with our free time? Are you up for a nap?" Marge handed Joey a clean frying pan to dry.

"Sure. We might be up late."

"Always good to be prepared. What time should I set my alarm for?"

"I don't know. Three?"

"Okay. I don't want to disturb you, so knock on my door when you're up."

Joey smirked. "I'll be up when you wake."

"Smarty pants." She went upstairs and lay on her bed, grateful for Millicent and saying a little prayer for Alan before her eyes closed and she was out.

⁕

Joey waited until four-thirty before he went upstairs. Marge's room was right at the top, so he left his walker at the bottom and held onto the banister. Knocking on her door, he put his ear against it and heard her rhythmical snore. "Marge." He knocked again then, receiving no reply, he opened the door a crack and let Fluster in. Chuckling, he knocked again. "Marge! Wakey wakey."

"Stop it Fluster! Joey, is that you?"

"Yes, it's time to get up."

"Did you let Fluster in here?"

"Yes, sorry. I needed assistance."

"What time is it?"

"Going on five. I'll start a new pot of coffee."

"Coming."

Marge entered the kitchen ten minutes later, with wild-looking hair and eyelashes that were no longer on her eyelids. She took the cup Joey offered her and sat down at the table.

"I'm always impressed with your napping ability Marge."

"I know. I'm sorry. When I lay down, my body thinks it's bedtime, no matter what time it is."

"Since we're supposed to be there at six, I thought you might want some time to wake up and get ready."

"You're right. I can't believe I slept that long. I'll just drink my coffee then get ready."

Joey smiled and sipped his coffee, eying Marge's errant eyelashes. When she had finished her coffee and gone upstairs, he fed Fluster and checked his phone. He was tired and glad to be going home after dinner; sleeping on someone else's sofa was not as restful as he had imagined.

Before long, Marge bounced into the kitchen, bun and eyelashes restored, and twirled around for his inspection.

"Have you been clothes shopping? I've noticed a few outfits I haven't seen before."

Nodding enthusiastically, Marge grinned. "I was wondering if you had noticed. You didn't say anything."

"I noticed. What do you call this color?"

"Chartreuse, I believe. The catalogue called it 'Paris green.' Do you like it?"

"Well, it's interesting. You do need some variety, right?"

"You don't like it." She frowned.

"I don't dislike it. It brings out the color of your eyes. I'm just used to seeing you in more vibrant colors." He smiled gently.

"Well, they can't all be your favorites, nor mine either. To tell the truth, I prefer bright colors as well."

"We can decorate you with red bows for Christmas. Are you ready to go?"

"Yes, I just need to feed Fluster and get bundled up."

"I already fed him. I'll warm up the UTV if you like."

"No, I'm ready. I think we should be careful on the ice."

"It's snowing again. Maybe that will help with traction."

Slipping and sliding down the walk to the UTV, Joey realized that Marge had been right. They saved each other from falling several times before getting safely into the vehicle.

As they drove past Millicent's house, he said, "They must have left already. The house is dark."

"They should have left the porch light on." She waved at Mrs. Waddle, Millicent's next-door neighbor, out walking her dog. "I wonder what the special is tonight. I'm hungry."

"Me too. I hope it's something hearty."

⸺ ⟨∞⟩ ⸺

Joey parked the UTV on the sidewalk, facing the wrong direction, so he could exit on a flat surface. Marge opened the door for him, the little bell ringing merrily. Helen said, "Sit anywhere you like. We're not very busy tonight."

"I hope you don't mind that I parked next to the door. This icy snow makes it hard for me to maneuver my walker."

"Don't worry. It's fine."

"We're supposed to meet James and Freida here. Have you seen them?"

"No, not yet."

Marge nodded and headed for a booth. "This seems more comfortable, doesn't it? And it's near the fire."

"The fire is nice when it's cold out. I wonder where they are. I didn't see them walking."

"Maybe they took a nap, too." Marge scrunched up her brow.

Arriving with menus, Helen said, "The special is steak and mashed potatoes with soup or salad. Did you want to wait?"

"No, we'll go ahead and order. What kind of soup is it?"

"Broccoli cheddar."

"I'll have the special with the salad and the steak well done."

"What kind of dressing?"

"Italian. And coffee."

"I'll have the same," Joey said, "except make my steak medium rare."

"And to drink?"

"I'll have coffee too."

"You two are always so easy." Helen smiled. "I'll be right back with the coffee."

Marge looked at the clock. "Do you think they're coming?"

"I have no idea. Unless they overslept, I would think they'd be here by now. Let's just enjoy our dinner and they can order when they arrive."

Chapter 33

James and Freida didn't show up at the Fireside, and on their way home, Marge pointed out that the lights in Millicent's house were still out. She wasn't too worried until Joey pulled up in his driveway and found Paws sitting on his front porch.

Joey opened his front door and turned off the alarm, as Marge and Paws looked around; well, Marge looked, and Paws sniffed.

Standing in the middle of the living room, Marge said, "We need to give this some thought. There is no way they would have left Paws outside by himself, unless he ran off, and he's never run off before; he loves Freida." She walked into the kitchen and saw two bags of perishables sitting on the table. "Something's wrong, Joey."

Joey, having trailed her into the kitchen, looked into the bags and felt the milk and butter. "This food isn't cold. It's been here a while."

"James said he would make an additional trip if they couldn't carry everything. What do you think transpired?"

"Maybe one of them had an accident and they had to go to the ER?"

"Will you call? I'm going to go down to Millicent's and see if they answer."

"Wait and I'll drive us over. I don't think you should go alone."

"I could text Petey while you call the hospital."

They both pulled out their phones. While Joey spoke to the receptionist at the hospital, Marge texted, "Petey, something is wrong at Millicent's house. James and Freida have disappeared, and Paws was outside. Could you come? We are going there now."

Joey disconnected and shook his head. Marge showed him her text. "Let's go," she said.

They got back into the UTV, leaving Paws inside Joey's house, and drove down the street.

Although someone had made an attempt at shoveling the walkway, it was still impassible for Joey's walker. "You stay here, and I'll take a look. Hopefully, Petey will be here soon."

"No, remember what you said about the ice? You take the walker, and I'll walk behind you for balance."

He looked determined, so Marge complied.

Once they reached the porch, Marge handed his walker back and then crawled to the front window. Joey got on his hands and knees and followed her, gently placing his hand on her head. "Your bun," he whispered, then he slowly raised his head so he could see over the windowsill.

The living room was dark and appeared empty, but he could see a faint light coming from the kitchen. Lowering his head, he whispered again, "Someone might be in the kitchen. There's a light on in there. Maybe we should have brought Paws."

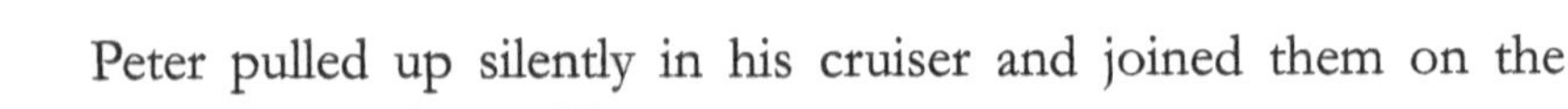

Peter pulled up silently in his cruiser and joined them on the porch. "What's going on?"

"We don't know," Marge said.

Peter knocked on the front door and waited, as Joey peeked through the window again. The light in the kitchen went out. Peter knocked again. "Stay here," he told Marge and Joey, then pulled out his radio and walked back to his cruiser.

Marge watched him walk away then said, "I'll be right back." Before Joey could stop her, she hopped off the side of the porch and waded through the snow to the back yard. She climbed over the chain-link fence and, staying close to the wall, quietly moved around the outside of the house.

She had to leave the shelter of the house a few times to veer around obstacles such as large shrubs, a wheelbarrow, and a ladder, but finally reached the back porch.

The problem was that to reach the French doors that led to the kitchen, she would have to cross the raised, wooden platform, which was covered in two feet of glistening snow. *Luckily my jacket is white. Maybe whoever is in there won't see me.*

She was about to crawl up the steps when a slender shadow approached the glass doors from the inside and peered out. *Freida!* she thought, then flinched when an arm grabbed her around the middle and pulled her away from the steps.

"That's not Freida," Peter said quietly.

"Who is it then?"

"I don't know. Backup's on the way. Stay very quiet. They might be armed."

"But James and Freida?"

"Is there another entrance to the house?"

"The garage."

"You need to stay out of the way. I don't want you to get hurt."

Marge frowned. The shadow inside had left the window. *Are James and Freida in the kitchen too? I must do something.*

Peter glared at her.

It's like he can read my mind.

"Go back around front."

"Should we bring Paws? He could act as a distraction."

"Just go wait with Joey in the UTV."

Marge was on her way back around the house when she noticed the ladder propped up against the side. She glanced around to see if anyone was watching, then began to climb.

The roof was a lot slicker than she expected, but she was determined to rescue her friends. Sliding slowly across the peak on her stomach, she tried to use as much of her body as possible for traction. When she was parallel to the terrace, there was no way for her to descend, except to slide.

With nothing to hold onto and worried about noise, she lowered herself as far as she could and let go.

Luckily, or not, her landing was softened by the jacuzzi. Unfortunately, the French windows were locked, and she was soaked through.

Shivering violently, she pulled out a hairpin and set to work on the lock. *I hope he can't hear all the noise I'm making. There!* The lock clicked open, and Marge slid into the room, quietly closing the doors behind her, and standing motionless to allow her eyes time to adjust.

When they did, she saw two pairs of eyes looking at her from across the room. "James? Freida?" she whispered. The eyes bobbed up and down. She crossed the room and knelt in front of their chairs. "Do you want me to try to pull the duct tape off your mouths? Or get your arms free and let you do it yourselves? It's going to hurt." James moved his hands and motioned with his head. "A knife or scissors would be helpful. Do you have anything?" James lifted his hip slightly. "Your pocket?" He nodded. "Excuse my hands, please."

Marge extracted a pocketknife and set to work freeing James first, then Freida. James then took the knife with him into the bathroom and cut a slit in the tape across his mouth.

"Better than nothing," he said in a whispered mumble. "The facial hair is going to be a problem."

Freida gestured to her own duct taped mouth. She gently took Marge's arm and made a quick, pulling gesture, so Marge nodded and took one end of the tape. "Pull the left side of your mouth taught," she whispered. Marge took the right side, holding the skin as taught as she could with her right hand, and quickly yanking the tape with her left. Freida's eyes teared, but she remained silent.

Giving Freida a hug, Marge took out her phone and texted Peter. "I'm upstairs with James and Freida. They are safe."

"Stay there," he texted back.

Peter couldn't believe his eyes. *That woman is going to give me a heart attack.* He was coordinating a break in and was actually glad to know the 'hostages' wouldn't be in the line of fire.

Three officers were prepared to enter the front door, and two, including Peter, were in the back, out of sight of the kitchen doors, waiting to enter once the perpetrator was distracted.

Peter gave the go signal and watched the perpetrator's head turn toward the kitchen door. He moved out of sight, so Peter approached the French doors and quickly picked the lock. He and Sergeant Holmes crept quietly through the kitchen and into the living room, where they found Deputy Bloom standing over the body of the 'handyman' from Rutherford Mansion.

Peter's brow furrowed. "Did you shoot him?"

Bloom shook his head in response.

"Locke? Come take a look at this."

Peter joined Sergeant Holmes in the kitchen, where the French doors were standing open and fresh footprints led away from the house, toward the back fence.

"Bloom," he called, "Go with Holmes and Surge. Follow these footprints. Sanders, call the chief and the ME."

After Holmes and Bloom left, Peter and Sanders searched the house, finding Marge with Freida and James in the master bedroom.

"Why are you soaking wet?" Peter asked her.

"The jacuzzi broke my landing."

"Let me get you something dry," Freida suggested.

"No, thank you, dear. I'll break out into hives if I wear any kind of natural fibers. Maybe you could just get me a towel to sit on."

Peter looked at James and Freida. "Are you two okay?"

"Yes, except for the duct tape on James' beard. How did you know what happened?"

"Aunt Marge saw your lights off and found Paws outside, so she called me."

"We're so lucky to have a friend like you." Freida smiled at Marge through belated tears. "We could have been here for weeks."

"Nonsense. No one would have ignored your absence for an extended period of time. Do you have some Vaseline or something you could put on your mouth? It looks painful."

"Yes. What do we do about James?" They both gazed at him in concern.

"I think I'll have to shave," he mumbled unhappily.

"Could I ask you some questions first?" Peter pulled out his notebook and a pen.

"Of course. Could we go downstairs, though? I want to get out of this room." Freida took James' hand.

"I'm afraid I'll need to ask you to stay here for now. There's a crime scene in the living room. Why don't you start at the beginning?"

"We gathered up our belongings, except for some perishable foods, and came over here with Paws, all excited to see Millicent's house. Then when we opened the front door, Paws bounded in ahead of us. We were taking off our coats, when a man came out of the kitchen with a gun.

"He made James put Paws outside and told us to go upstairs. Then he taped us up and left. The house was quiet, and we didn't know where he was or what he was doing. We couldn't talk to each other or anything. I couldn't believe it when Marge came in from the balcony. She was in shadow, but I recognized her bun."

"He didn't say anything to you about why he was here? Or ask you why you were here?"

"No, nothing."

"Could you identify him in a lineup?"

"Oh, yes. Not only because he was very close when he was taping us up, but we also saw him at the pub."

James wasn't saying much but he nodded emphatically.

"What about his partner?"

"We didn't see anyone else, but we heard a gunshot. Have you caught them?"

"The 'caretaker' is dead, and his partner ran. We're looking for him."

Freida shivered. "You won't leave until you find him, will you?"

"No, someone will stay here with you." Peter stood. "I might have some more questions later, but I'll let you get on with things for now, and I'll keep you informed."

"If we order food, could you bring it up to us?" Marge asked. "And can Joey come up?"

"Yes, I'll have him bring the food when it gets here."

Watching Peter leave, Marge said, "The perishables left at Joey's are spoiled. What are you in the mood for?"

"Chinese?"

"That sounds good. I'll call the Jade Palace."

When she put the phone down, after ordering half the menu, she studied Freida carefully. "Has this incident put you off staying here?"

Tilting her head slightly, Freida thought for a moment. "It's funny, but no. The mansion was different because we didn't know who the intruder was or how he was getting in. And the house is so big, with all those secret passages. This time, the police are here, and we'll know if anyone's in the house." She wrinkled her nose. "Does that make sense?"

"Yes, it's an entirely different situation."

Marge heard Joey thumping up the stairs and went to give him a hand. "Petey should have helped."

"He's knee deep in the crime scene. I hear James might need some help.

"I brought your luggage with me."

James stood and mumbled his thanks, gesturing toward the bathroom, so Joey followed him and shut the door. When they came out again, James was almost unrecognizable.

"Wow," Freida exclaimed. "I had no idea how handsome you were under all that hair. I'll have to fight other women off with a stick."

He laughed. "You like me beardless?"

"I love you no matter what you look like, but this look is very attractive."

"You can thank Joey because I was dragging my feet. Are we ready to eat?"

"Marge ordered enough food for an army."

Chapter 34

Sergeant Holmes and Deputy Bloom returned with Surge. "We lost him. The footprints ended in an alley where we found fresh tire tracks, possibly Gary's Tacoma. What's going on here?"

"The ME said time of death was likely about two hours ago. Cause of death was a gunshot wound to the head, meant to look like suicide but the body was moved after death." They approached the scene and noticed Marge sitting on the stairs, watching.

Lloyd looked up, narrowing his eyes, and glancing at Peter, he said, "I should have known."

"She called me." Peter hoped he wouldn't get blamed for her presence.

"Yes, yes. The murder magnet. Fill me in on what happened."

Peter explained the situation and waited for the chief's input.

Marge cleared her throat. "I don't wish to interrupt, but have you considered approaching it from an alternative perspective?"

Both men stared at her.

"We only have Nicole's story about her relationship with the brothers, her feelings, her loyalties, who did what."

Lloyd gazed at her. "You may have something there, Ms. Bumfuzzle. Do you think she'll return to the mansion?"

"That's where her paintings are. Has anyone called the hospital?"

"Locke?"

Peter was shocked at this turnabout in the chief's attitude. *He might think Aunt Marge is a murder magnet, but he sure seems to be taking her seriously.* "I'm on it."

He alerted Bloom and pulled out his phone, leaving the house with a backward glance at his aunt.

205

Not wanting to overstay her welcome, Marge returned upstairs to resume her consumption of Chinese food. Joey, Freida, and James had finished eating, and they had laid out some extra paper plates for any of the officers who needed a snack.

Joey watched her eat. "What were you talking to Peter and the chief about?"

"Just a little idea I had."

"You're not sharing?"

She smiled and popped another forkful of cashew chicken into her mouth.

Peter radioed his officers at the mansion before driving to the hospital. Surprised to see him, the officer on duty gave Peter an update.

"Ms. Reid left for a few hours. She said she was going to the cafeteria but was gone for a long time. Mr. Marshall is very weak but is expected to recover. I hope you don't mind, but I requested that the hospital security department install a small camera and listening device while Ms. Reid was gone."

"Does Mr. Marshall know about them?"

"He appeared to be sleeping when they were installed."

"Who is monitoring them?"

"The security team."

"How long has Ms. Reid been back?"

"About half an hour."

"How do I get to the security department?"

"Take the elevator to the basement and turn right."

"Thanks."

Peter left Bloom at the door and made his way to the security office. They let him in and showed him the video stream.

Nicole was sitting in a chair by Gary's bed, watching him sleep.

When he opened his eyes, he frowned at her. "Why?"

"I think you know why. You got out of jail and made me a prisoner. I've been living in a windowless dungeon without friends or money or transportation."

"You had your art. And Larry." His voice was a whisper, so weak he could hardly be heard.

"Where do you have the bug?" Peter asked, leaning forward.

"It's on the side of the nightstand."

"Can you turn up the sound?"

"No, it's up as high as it will go."

After a pause, Nicole said, "I don't even like Larry. Are you going to die?"

"Probably. I love you, Nicole. All I ever wanted was to be with you."

"Maybe you should have tried a little harder."

"If I make it, I promise to do better."

"You aren't going to make it."

Gary studied her silently then looked over at their sleeping son. "He'll be alone."

"He always has been."

"I'm sorry. I really screwed things up." He closed his eyes, and his breathing gradually became more even and shallow.

Nicole glanced at her son and picked up a pillow.

"Now!" Peter shouted into his radio. "Get in there now!"

Bloom and the guard burst into the room. "Put the pillow down, Ms. Reid. It's all over."

Nicole continued holding the pillow over Gary's face, as if she hadn't heard, so Deputy Bloom approached and removed it from her hands. He handcuffed her and said, "Nicole Reid Marshall, I am arresting you for the murders of Douglas Taft, Fred Dawson, and Lawrence Marshall, and for the attempted murder of Gary Marshall and Sayuri O'Donnell. You have the right to remain silent..."

"I didn't kill Douglas. He was supposed to rescue me!"

Gary opened his eyes and gaped at her in disbelief. "I thought maybe in the heat of the moment, but I never thought…" A tear slid down his cheek.

Peter shook hands with the security chief and went upstairs to accompany Bloom and Nicole to the station.

They sat at a small table in the interview room, and Peter began the recording. He slid a piece of paper and a pen across the table. "For the record, could you please write out your full legal name?"

She wrote her name and slid it back to him.

"For the record, this interview is with Nicole Reid Marshall. Would you prefer to be addressed as Ms. Reid or Mrs. Marshall?"

"Ms. Reid, please, or Nicole."

"Very well, Ms. Reid, let's start at the beginning. Where were you living when you found out your husband, Gary Marshall, had escaped from prison?"

"I was living in a hotel near the hospital."

"And whose idea was it to move into the basement of Rutherford Mansion?"

"Larry was running the pub and Gary needed a place to hide, so he said he would run the pub and Larry could take care of me. He told us about the mansion."

"You weren't asked?"

"No, I was told."

"How did you get along with Lawrence?"

"He was okay." She shrugged.

"Why did he beat you and tape you to the chair in the old stone hut?"

"He didn't. That was Gary. He's a scary guy."

"Why didn't you let someone know?"

Nicole looked at Peter, then at Dennis, and went to turn the wedding band that was no longer on her finger.

"When the brothers drove to the stone hut, did they pick you up on the way, or did you meet them there?"

"I don't know what you mean."

"You were there, the officer who was killed, recorded the whole thing."

"I." Nicole opened her mouth then shut it again. "Larry told me to come and to stay hidden."

"Why?"

"I don't know. Maybe to prove to Gary that he hurt me or that I wasn't at the station." She shook her head.

"There were two guns at the scene and only one was found."

Nicole didn't comment.

"Where did the other one go?"

"I guess Larry took it."

"Was he wearing gloves?"

"I don't remember."

"Why did you kill Larry?"

"I didn't!"

Peter lifted a brow. "You were at the house. No one else was there. Your footprints were in the snow. Do you have another explanation?"

"He told me to meet him there, but he was dead when I arrived."

"Have you found the treasure?"

"What?"

"The treasure mentioned in the journal."

"No."

"Then why did you kill them?"

"I didn't." Her voice was shrill. "I changed my mind. I want a lawyer."

Peter stood. "Let her have her phone call then put her in a cell. I need to check on some things."

Chapter 35

The sun was rising when Marge answered Peter's knock. "Can we talk?"

"Of course. Would you like something to eat? You look weary."

He nodded and followed her into Millicent's kitchen. Greeting Joey, James, and Freida, he sat with them at the table and accepted the plate of left-over Chinese food Marge offered him. "I think I might be too tired to eat. I don't know how you keep going, Aunt Marge. You're like the energizer bunny."

"I think I'm becoming accustomed to thirty-six-hour shifts." She smiled.

"We've arrested Nicole, but there are still a lot of details I don't understand."

"What led to your arrest?"

"She tried to kill Gary this evening."

Marge nodded. "She returned to the hospital. I think if you lay out all your evidence, her lawyer will advise her to plea bargain, and you might finally hear her story.

"There were clues, even before the murders. When she broke in to find the book, for example. She must have been the person who assaulted Deputy Bloom because the person on the UTV would have taken a while to traverse the tunnel.

"Either she hit him from behind, or one of the brothers entered with her, then left in the UTV. I don't know if anyone else was in the passages or not. Have you interviewed Gary?"

"Not yet. The doctor thought he'd had enough excitement for one night."

"He might elucidate her impetuses."

"I did hear them talking before she tried to smother him."

James leaned forward and said, "You're sure no one else is involved? We're no longer in any danger?"

"You're safe enough here. We'll speak with Hugh about the mansion. For now, you should all try to get some sleep."

"Can we sleep in your house one more night, Joey?" Freida asked tremulously. "I thought I was okay here, but I'm not."

"Yes. Let's all head back. Marge looks like she's about to drop."

They locked up Millicent's house, and Peter dismissed the deputy on duty before saying goodnight.

James and Freida walked wearily back to Joey's house, and Joey drove Marge home in the UTV. She was partially dry by that time but shivered in the icy wind.

"Would you like me to build a fire?" Joey asked with concern.

"No, I'll just change and retire for the evening. I am extremely fatigued." She opened the door to a scowling feline. "Poor Fluster. I'm sorry about your disrupted schedule. Let's get you something to eat."

Fluster didn't even bother to yowl. He watched her walk into the kitchen and followed when he was sure she was prepared to feed him.

Once he was fed, Marge mumbled, "goodnight," and headed upstairs. She put on her pajamas and let her hair down, placing a towel over her pillow and climbing into bed, but although she was exhausted, she lay with her eyes open, thinking about Nicole and her situation. *How desperate would she have to be to have killed all those people? Had she been planning it all along? What kind of person is she?*

Marge finally closed her eyes and prayed. "Lord, please help me see the truth and allow me to rest. I'm so tired. Amen," she mumbled before she fell into a deep sleep.

She slept all day and through the night, waking suddenly the next morning. She sat up in bed and said, "Where's the money?"

She got dressed and ran downstairs to talk to Joey.

Joey looked up from the book he was reading when Marge descended. "Good morning."

"We need to ask Petey about the money."

"The money? Was that something you dreamt about? Are you hungry?"

"I am hungry. I'm famished. But I need to talk to Petey."

"I made pancake batter, so I'll make you some while you call him."

Marge nodded absently and pulled out her phone, so Joey went into the kitchen to cook pancakes.

When Marge joined him, he indicated a plate of pancakes, which she carried to the table before pouring them each a cup of coffee.

They sat down and Marge eyed the pancakes. "If I don't remain vigilant, your culinary skills will surpass my own. These look scrumptious." She took a bite and smiled.

"I'm glad you like them."

"What day is it, anyway?"

"It's Thursday. You asked me that last Thursday." Joey chuckled.

"The Christmas party was scheduled for this weekend."

There was a knock on the door, so Marge went to answer it, returning with Peter.

"Would you like some pancakes?" Joey asked. "I made plenty of batter."

"Sure. Thanks." Peter sat down and accepted a cup of coffee and a plate. "What did you want to talk to me about, Aunt Marge?"

"Where is all the money Mr. Taft paid for Nicole's paintings?"

"I don't know."

"Are you able to uncover that information?"

"I can try. What's the idea?"

"There is a trove of money somewhere and the supposed treasure. Someone will be very rich. It wasn't Nicole who stabbed Mark, and I don't believe she killed Douglas. So, who was the culprit?"

"I'll look into it." Peter put his fork down.

"Thanks for breakfast. I have to go."

Marge watched him as he went, then turned her attention to Joey. "What's on the agenda today?"

"Well, I'm pleased to announce that most of the snow melted yesterday and today is supposed to be above freezing as well. We can probably go see what's happening at the mansion."

"I answered the door and didn't heed the weather! I typically love snow, but this week has been excessive. I am anticipating a walk."

"Me too," Joey said heartily. "I wonder what James and Freida are up to."

"Why don't we go find out… if we can cross the street. Did you see them yesterday?"

"No, but I spoke to James on the phone, and he was talking about getting back to work on the renovations."

Marge pulled their coats out of the hall closet and handed Joey his. He took his coat and eyed her carefully. "Are you leaving your hair down today?"

"Oh. No, I think I'd better restrain it. Could you feed Fluster for me?" She ran back upstairs, so Joey fed the cat and poured himself another cup of coffee.

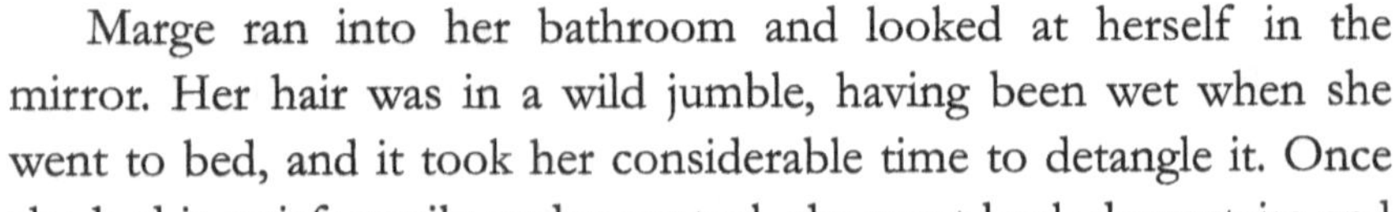

Marge ran into her bathroom and looked at herself in the mirror. Her hair was in a wild jumble, having been wet when she went to bed, and it took her considerable time to detangle it. Once she had it satisfactorily under control, she went back downstairs and apologized for making Joey wait.

"That's okay. I had another cup of coffee and talked to James. He and Freida will meet us over at the mansion."

"Excellent. I want to revisit the basement." Marge put on her coat and opened the front door, to find patches of green grass on her lawn.

Smiling, she lifted her face to the sun and spread her arms. "Oh, sun, how I do love thee."

Joey chuckled and unlocked the UTV. "Come on, sun maiden."

Skipping with joy, Marge joined him, and they drove the short distance to the Rutherford house. "I wonder if we should have conveyed provisions. We do have a penchant for working long hours."

"We won't be staying that long today. I promise." Joey parked in the circular drive. "Look, the construction crew is back."

"I feel like we've been absent for a week."

"Not quite that long." Joey winked.

Hugh exited the house with a smile and held out his hand to shake Joey's. "It's been a while. How have you two been?"

"Frequently sleep deprived. How about you?" Joey shook his hand.

"Just sitting around waiting for the snow to melt. I'm glad we can get back to work."

"Are James and Freida here?"

"Not yet, but we have some volunteers who brought food and seem happy to be back. They're upstairs, and the crew is working on the third floor."

"Have the secret passages been sealed?"

"Yes, that was our first task, yesterday. We can always open them if we want a 'haunted B&B' theme in the future, but for now I think we'll all feel better knowing the house is secure.

"I'm sure Freida will feel better now." Joey nodded. "We won't keep you. Let's go see what the others are up to," he said to Marge. She was already walking toward the front entrance, so he trotted to catch up to her. "Where's the fire?"

"No fire, I'm just excited to see what we've missed." They went upstairs to find Pastor Greg, Harriet, and Millicent. "Good morning!" Marge said. "No one has turned into an icicle?"

"We all made it through the storm. I'm so glad to be out of the house," Millicent was perched on a stool with a paintbrush.

"I got stuck at the rectory," Harriet said. "So much for propriety." Greg blushed and she laughed. "It was a lot less lonely than being home alone."

James and Freida walked in just then and said good morning.

"Where have you two been?" Pastor Greg asked.

"We stayed at Joey's house for a few nights," Freida said.

"I thought you were going to stay at my house."

"We were, but… no one told you?"

"Told me what?"

"Oh dear." Marge grimaced.

Thinking it was lucky that Millicent was of the sensible variety, Marge listened to Freida's retelling of their kidnapping and the murder of Lawrence Marshall.

Another type of woman might have sold the house at once, but Millicent was focused on Freida's safety. "That must have been terrifying. I'm so relieved that they've caught the culprit."

"Petey said they are deploying the cleaners," Marge said.

Millicent nodded. "So, what are your plans?"

"We've brought our things with us. James said the construction crew has sealed off all the entrances, both inside and out, so we won't have any more uninvited guests." Freida gave a little shudder.

"Since you are back home," Millicent said, "are we still having a Christmas party this weekend?"

Freida looked at James, then at Marge. "I don't really see how we could on such short notice."

"Easy peasy. Let's have it Sunday night, so Pastor Greg can make an announcement in church. It will be great fun." Millicent's eyes were twinkling.

"I guess we'd better get back to work then," Joey grinned.

"We don't have too much to do in here," James said.

"Let's get busy then."

Marge put her arm through Freida's. "You and I should re-examine the basement."

"I don't know. It still seems spooky."

"That's why we need to go. Hugh can come with us if you like."

Marge took her to find Hugh and he unlocked the basement door.

Walking from room to room, observing the contents of the basement and trying to imagine Nicole and Lawrence's daily lives, Marge noticed details she had missed on her first visit.

The spring was evidently used as a bath, as towels and sundries were stored nearby. The studio was Nicole's domain; Lawrence likely banned from entrance. Marge looked around carefully at the contents, her eye drawn to a large bookcase filled with an eclectic assortment of ancient tomes. Would Nicole have been interested in these titles?

Surprised, Marge caught sight of 'The Prophet,' by Kahlil Gibran, resting on the bottom shelf. Bending, she pulled it from between Mark Twain and Dickens, thinking she might like to give it a read, and as she recalled the quote in Abraham Rutherford's journal, her eyes grew wide with understanding.

She flipped through the book, searching for the quotation, and found $100 bills inserted between the pages. Setting down the book, she picked up another, and another. She pulled out her phone and texted Peter.

Chapter 36

That evening, Freida and James joined Marge and Joey for dinner at the Fireside café. They were seated around a table in the back enjoying a pre-dinner drink, when the little bell tinkled, and Peter walked in. He approached their table and said, "I thought I might find you here. Mind if I join you?"

"Please do," Freida said. "Have you eaten?"

"I can't stay. I just wanted to give you an update."

They all looked at him expectantly.

"I had an interesting day. Thanks to Marge, we know where the money went. I spoke to Hugh and will let him decide if he wants to dig up the pool or not. Then I went to the hospital and interviewed Gary Marshall.

"He didn't want to talk at first, but I reminded him that he was going back to prison, and that Nicole had tried to kill him, twice, so he told me their story.

"He was convicted of manslaughter when he beat a man to death after he made an aggressive pass at Nicole while they were out one night. When he escaped from prison, with his brother's help, they came up with the plan of switching places. Nicole was most concerned about little Alan at the time and just went along with things, but as time went by, she became angry and resentful.

"Lawrence gradually fell in love with Nicole and began creating a wedge between them. For example, he told Gary that Nicole had told the police about him and let them search the basement where she and Lawrence lived.

"Gary, angry at her betrayal, drug her to the stone hut and secured her to a chair while he went to find his brother. When he returned, he found Nicole gone and assumed Lawrence had released her."

Helen brought their dinners and tried to maintain an upbeat professional demeanor with limited success. "Can I get you anything else?"

"Not right now," Marge said. "Thank you."

She quickly returned to the kitchen, and Marge took a bite of her dinner. "Delicious."

"Fergus has outdone himself." Joey chuckled at the name the chef shared with Marge's mouse.

"Did Gary tell you what happened the day he was shot?" Marge asked.

"He did. He and Lawrence drove to the old stone hut and got out of the truck. They were arguing about Nicole, and Gary drew his gun. He said that he hadn't intended to shoot his brother, but Nicole appeared in the entrance to the hut and shot him. He didn't know why she was there or where she had gotten a gun, but when he fell, she approached him and took his. He thought he must have lost consciousness, because the next thing he remembered, there were police everywhere and he was being loaded into an ambulance."

"I imagine Nicole assumed that Gary would die, so she went to take care of Lawrence while everyone thought she was at the hospital. Did you find out if she's left-handed?" Marge took a few bites and a sip of her drink, to catch up with the others.

"She is, and Lawrence was not. That was her big mistake. She shot him in the left side of the head and put the gun in his left hand, letting it drop and setting the scene for a suicide. The ME wasn't fooled, because he could tell the body had been moved, but the left-handed scene pointed right to Nicole."

"It almost seems too obvious," Joey said. "If you had another suspect, I would guess she was being framed."

"If she had killed him and departed immediately, you wouldn't have any clues. It was snowing, and the snow might have masked her footprints.

"I wonder why she staged such an elaborate scene." Marge frowned.

"I'll ask her when I interview her again. Perhaps she was just in over her head and panicked."

"Yes, panic can cause people to do some strange things."

"Did Gary say anything about Douglas?"

"He said that Lawrence killed Douglas because he thought he was buying Nicole's paintings behind his back which, based on the cash Nicole was hiding, was probably true. Of course, he mistakenly stabbed Mark and tried to kill Douglas after he was already dead, so he wasn't exactly a success."

"And Sayuri?"

"He said Nicole found her sneaking around in the basement and hit her over the head. According to Gary, it was an accident, and she begged him to help her get rid of the body. Unless she confesses, I'm not sure we can ever prove that."

"I have a hunch she'll confess." Marge said.

"Well, I'd better get back to work." Peter stood.

"Will you be attending James and Freida's make-up party on Sunday evening?"

"I wouldn't miss it for the world. May I invite Sergeant Holmes?"

"You can invite anyone you like. Is that the young lady with the dog named Surge?" Freida asked.

"Yes, but I think she will be able to attend without her canine partner."

"She's welcome to bring him, as long as he doesn't try to arrest Paws."

Peter chuckled. "I'll let her know. Anyway, I have to get going. I'll see you on Sunday, if not before." He rose and left the restaurant.

Helen returned to the table. "Can I get you another drink or dessert?"

"No, I think we're fine," Freida said.

"Well, maybe another whiskey," Marge said.

"And a piece of pie," James added.

"Right. Let's start at the beginning," Helen said, pulling out her order pad. They all laughed and put in their orders.

The meal was enjoyable, and James and Freida asked for one more night at Joey's, so after dinner they all headed back to Holly Lane.

Marge, feeling festive on Sunday morning, dressed in her cerise pantsuit and had breakfast nearly ready when Joey entered the kitchen.

"Good morning. You look lovely. Maybe you should have saved that outfit for the party. It's very festive."

"I think I might be able to wear it to the party too, as long as I don't have any food-related mishaps."

"Should I wear my fancy duds this morning too?"

"You should wear something warm, so your joints don't ache. Have a seat. I have something yummy for you."

Joey sat and lifted an eyebrow, then grinned when he saw what was for breakfast. "My favorite. What did I do to deserve this?"

"I found the steak and the tin of biscuits in the freezer and felt inspired." She poured them each a cup of coffee and joined him at the table. "We have enough for leftovers, if you want a repeat at lunch time."

"Are we supposed to take something to the party tonight?"

"Yes, a dessert or a bottle. I thought I might bake a cake this afternoon."

"We don't have to help with the decorations?"

"I don't believe they were removed. Furthermore, we might be desirous of a respite beforehand; you know how once we arrive, we seem unable to depart."

"You do have a point." Joey cut off a piece of his steak, cooked medium rare, just as he liked it, and popped it in his mouth, almost swooning from the delicious flavor. "Marge," he mumbled as he chewed, "this is so good."

Marge, busy sopping up her egg with a buttered biscuit, smiled and said, "This is a special occasion."

Eyes twinkling, Joey said, "It's Christmas eve, and I might be able to move back home tonight."

Pastor Greg stood in the vestibule greeting his parishioners as they arrived, visibly pleased with the turnout. Harriet, standing by his side, smiled at Marge and Joey. "We're glad you could make it this morning." A hint of Harriet's sometimes sarcastic personality snuck through before she carefully tucked it away.

Shaking Joey's hand, the pastor said, "Good morning. A lovely turnout today," then turned to the next person in line.

"Where shall we sit this morning, Marge?"

Scanning the sanctuary, Marge found Millicent, sitting next to Mrs. Waddle. "Let's sit over there with Millicent."

"Oh, good morning, Marge, Joey, will you be attending the party this evening?" she asked as she gave Mrs. Waddle a nudge and they scooted to the left.

"Indubitably. Good morning, Mrs. Waddle."

"Good morning, dear. It's good to see you. That snow was something else, wasn't it? I feel like I've been confined for weeks."

The pianist began to play, and everyone stood. Marge loved Christmas songs, and she sang enthusiastically, if slightly off key.

When they sat again, Joey nudged her and whispered, "Peter's here."

"Where?" Marge whipped her head around, setting her immense bun lurching.

"Shh. Marge. You're going to hurt someone with that bun. He's in the back corner. Just pretend you don't see him. I think he's trying to remain incognito."

"But he never comes."

"He's usually working."

Harriet approached the pulpit and opened her Bible. "Our first reading this morning is Psalm 34:18." She quietly cleared her throat and read. *The Lord is close to the brokenhearted and saves those who are crushed in spirit.*"

She paused and found the second passage. "Our second reading is from John 16:33. *These things I have spoken unto you, that in me ye might have peace. In the world ye shall have tribulation: but be of good cheer; I have overcome the world.*" She closed her Bible and said, "The Word of the Lord."

"Thanks be to God," the congregation intoned.

Pastor Greg approached the pulpit and said, "Let us pray." He bowed his head and prayed, "Lord, our community has experienced loss and tribulation during recent weeks, and we look to you for solace. We pray that you fill us with your peace and help us to forgive and to heal."

Chapter 37

Peter, who rarely attended church, paid close attention to the sermon that morning and left during the final hymn to avoid having to socialize. After interviewing Nicole, his heart was heavy. She showed no remorse or even concern over Sergeant Dawson's death. He meant nothing to her; just someone who appeared at the wrong time and place.

Stopping at his apartment to change into more comfortable clothes and grab a snack, he then drove to the stone hut and placed the folding chair in the clearing where he could see the place Dawson fell. He sat there a long time, letting his mind empty of thoughts and feelings, until gradually, there in the still forest, he thought he could feel the presence of God.

As the sun began to set, filling the sky with vibrant pink and orange, a car pulled into the clearing. Peter glanced up to see Tanya Holmes approaching. She sat on the ground, next to his chair, but said nothing. Sitting together silently, they watched dusk turn to darkness, until Peter turned to her. "Thank you," he said quietly.

She nodded, her eyes glistening in the dim light.

Peter stood and held out his hand to help her up. "Would you like to accompany me to a Christmas party?"

"I'm not really dressed for it, but yes."

"I don't think there are any requirements, but we can change first if you like."

"Do we have time?"

"We'll make time. We're supposed to take something too."

"I know. I made cookies."

"Perfect." Peter smiled at her.

"Have you found peace?" she asked quietly.

"Yes, I believe I have. I will tell you about it sometime, if you like, once I can articulate it. I'll pick you up in half an hour. Is that okay?"

"Yes, I'll be ready."

Returning home, Peter searched the back of his closet for his tuxedo. *If Tanya's dressing up, I should wear something to do her justice.* He dressed quickly and drove to her house, not wanting to keep her waiting. When she answered his knock, his breath caught in his throat. Her dress was form-fitting, with a little flair at the bottom, and covered in green sequins. Her hair was pinned up, with curled tendrils framing her face. "You are stunning," he whispered.

Blushing becomingly, Tanya smiled and said, "You clean up pretty nicely too, Sergeant."

Peter helped her into her coat and took her elbow, opening her car door and making sure she was comfortable.

The Christmas party was a smaller version of the housewarming party and ended on a much happier note. James and Freida greeted their guests at the door, looking relaxed and content. Mark Stubbs and Freida's mother, Caroline, had arrived together and seemed to be getting along. Pastor Greg and Harriet were all smiles, and Millicent sparkled.

Joey found Marge sitting on a chair at the edge of the dance floor, looking deep in thought. "Penny for your thoughts," he said, sitting next to her.

"I was just observing all our friends enjoying themselves and thinking about what Sayuri expressed at the hospital. We really are fortunate to be surrounded by so many wonderful friends."

"I am particularly lucky to have a best friend like you."

"Where is she, anyway? I expected her to be here."

"She decided to go home. She asked me to thank you."

Marge looked at her feet. "I was afraid you would remarry her and move away."

"Marge." He shook his head with a grin. "If I wanted to marry someone, it would be you. You're my other half... and you make awesome pancakes. Come on. Let's dance."

He stood and took her hand, leading her onto the dance floor with one hand on his walker. He stopped in the center of the ballroom and did a 'Saturday Night Fever' pose.

"Oh, my," she said, laughing, as the Bee Gees began to play.

When Joey finally pulled the UTV up to the curb in front of Marge's house he said, "Can I show you your Christmas present tonight?"

Marge looked surprised.

"It's after midnight, so it's technically Christmas."

"Only if I can give you yours too."

Joey grinned. "Come with me."

Marge followed him into her house and out through the French doors in the kitchen. Walking out onto her patio she stopped and watched as Joey folded back a tarp with a giant red bow, then she gasped. "Joey!"

There, built into her raised, wooden porch, was a beautiful jacuzzi.

"Your wish is my command." He grinned.

"Should we get in now?"

"Maybe tomorrow, when we've had a little rest."

"It's calling to me." She looked at it longingly, then looked at Joey. "Thank you so much! It's the best present ever." She hugged him. "You still have to open your present. Come back inside; it's by the tree."

Returning to the living room, Marge told Joey to sit on the sofa while she went to the tree and picked up a package he hadn't noticed before. Handing it to him she said, "This is a present for both of us."

"Kind of like the jacuzzi," he said.

Marge sat down next to him as he began to unwrap the box. Inside, he found three balls of wadded up tissue paper. He removed the first one and unwrapped an ornament shaped like a palm tree. The second was shaped like a hula dancer and the third, a tiny airplane. Finally, lying at the bottom of the box, he found a large, padded envelope. He pried it open and pulled out the contents, his eyes widening in surprise. He stared at it for a moment then grinned. "We won't have to pretend anymore."

"We can still pretend when we return."

"It's for a whole month?"

"Is that acceptable?"

"Absolutely. Nothing could be better than hanging out with you on a tropical beach in the middle of February. I wish I had thought of it."

Marge smiled happily. "Merry Christmas, Joey."

"Merry Christmas." He hugged her fiercely and silently thanked God again for bringing her into his life.

Alice Kanaka has been reading everything she could get her hands on since she could hold a book and writing stories about the world around her. Her youth was a series of moves across the United States, accompanied by her sibling sidekick and her books.

After studying abroad in England and Spain and a short stint working for Club Med, Alice packed her bag once more and went to teach in Japan. Her story continues along the same vein, adding languages, kids and cats into the mix. Open one of her mysteries to see the world through her eyes. You won't be disappointed.

HTTPS://AliceKanaka.com

If you'd like to see more of Alice's adventures, make sure to check out her **travel blog!**

https://ExploringWithAlice.com

Sign up for Alice's mailing list to get notifications and to be entered in a monthly raffle!

<u>Other Titles:</u>
Trouble at the Buckeye Festival
The Cardinal & The Crow
The Cardinal, The Fat Boy & The Flamingo
The Cardinal & The Hawk